the boy

Also by Lara Santoro
Mercy

the boy

a novel

lara santoro

Little, Brown and Company

New York Boston London

Copyright © 2013 by Lara Santoro

Little, Brown and Company
Hachette Book Group
237 Park Avenue, New York, NY 10017
littlebrown.com

First Edition: January 2013

Little, Brown and Company is a division of Hachette Book Group, Inc. The Little, Brown name and logo are trademarks of Hachette Book Group, Inc.

The publisher is not responsible for websites (or their content) that are not owned by the publisher.

The Hachette Speakers Bureau provides a wide range of authors for speaking events. To find out more, go to hachettespeakersbureau.com or call (866) 376-6591.

Library of Congress Cataloging-in-Publication Data

Santoro, Lara.
  The boy : a novel / Lara Santoro. — 1st ed.
    p. cm.
  ISBN 978-0-316-20623-5
  1. Single women—Fiction. 2. Self-realization in women—Fiction. 3. May-December romances—Fiction. 4. Motherhood—Fiction. I. Title.
  PS3619.A596B69 2013
  813'.6—dc23   2012020388

10 9 8 7 6 5 4 3 2 1

RRD-C

Printed in the United States of America

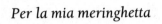

Per la mia meringhetta

the boy

Chapter One

She could not remember meeting him. She tried, sifting through the early hours of that first night of summer, to retrieve the instant when their eyes first met, their hands first touched, but found that she could not. The boy had slipped into her life sideways: one minute he was not there, the next he was seated to her right, asking her things.

Yet there had to have been an introduction. They were at his father's house and Richard Strand was not one to shed formalities, not even for his son. She'd gotten there late, there had been a small multitude milling about with drinks already, but how could it be that this boy—this dark son, this cauldron of want—had failed to register?

They'd been celebrating the arrival of summer with drinks of mint and sugar and way too much hard stuff. Anna had secured a stool in the kitchen and had been sufficiently entertained by the flow of conversation to stay put. Kitchens, with their innate goodness, their earthly balance, exercised a vast magnetic pull on Anna at parties, Richard Strand's kitchen more so than most because of why the man cooked, the reason why his pans were blackened, his cutting boards cracked, his wooden spoons split. Richard Strand cooked for his children, so they could bite into his love, so they could taste the texture of his longing for them. He cooked for his older sons, whose comings and goings were notoriously hectic, and for his younger ones, whose small, cluttered lives he shared only in part.

On her stool, mildly drunk, Anna had gotten started on the subject of a movie actor whose face had always frightened her.

"It's the plasticity of it," she told her friend Mia. Mia knocked back half a glass of wine, considered the remaining half with mounting animosity, and said, "Plasticity?"

"Yeah. It scares me."

She paused, thinking of how to better convey the depth of her discomfort, when to her left someone said, "And you don't like that."

She turned, struck by the quietness of the affirmation, and there, sitting on a stool, was the boy, Richard Strand's firstborn son.

"Sorry?" she said.

"And you don't like that."

"No. I don't."

The boy kept his clear eyes on hers. "What else don't you like?"

Anna took a closer look. The boy wore dark, baggy clothes

so there was no discerning the profile of his body, yet Anna could tell, simply by the way he sat, that it must be a good one. She raised her eyes to his with calculated slowness and found to her surprise that they were free of fear, free of pretense, free of the myriad layers stretched by age over the human eye.

"What else don't I like?" she murmured almost to herself. "I don't know. I don't know what else I don't like."

"I do," the boy said, his eyes on her mouth.

A dark current ran up her spine. She'd come across that look before.

"You don't like cheap white wine," he said.

"Cheap white wine? Show me someone who does."

"You don't like having your back to the room."

It was true, Anna never sat with her back to any room. It seemed crazy to her, a wholly unnecessary duel with the forces of chaos.

"You prefer the company of women but you attract the company of men. You'd rather drink than eat your calories. You wish you'd never quit smoking."

She crossed and uncrossed her legs, stared stonily ahead.

"You drive a truck you don't need. You're capable of wearing the exact same outfit three days in a row. No use denying it: I've seen you. You're always at the video store paying late fees. Netflix—the entire phenomenon, the great revolution—seems to have passed you by."

She shot to her feet. "Have you been following me?"

Mia leaned in. "Has he been following you?"

The boy propped his elbows on the counter behind him. "I don't follow people," he said. "It's not my thing. I watch. I observe. I gather information. I draw conclusions I keep to myself. I've got shit on everyone in this room."

"Oh brother," said Mia. "I'm leaving," but then a realization struck her and she pointed a finger at the boy. "Weren't you in college? Doing something useful?"

"Expensive. Not useful."

"Oh brother," Mia said, and pushed her way out of the room.

"What's her problem?" the boy asked, his voice mellow.

"None that I can see."

"You two are always at the coffee shop in the morning. You're always talking."

"That's what people do in coffee shops. They talk."

"Every day for the past two months. Endless conversations. What do you have to talk about?"

"The reasons we didn't drop out of college."

The boy smiled and shook his head. "Every day. For the past two months."

"Two months? You've been back two months? How come I've never seen you?"

"You don't wear your glasses. You spend half your life trying to put things into focus. You should wear your glasses."

Anna sat back down. The population density in the kitchen had risen sharply; people packed like sardines were pressing in from all sides.

"So. What do you do with all this 'shit'?"

He drained half of his beer. "There's only one worthwhile application. Not two, not three, not four: one. Want to guess what it is?"

Anna crossed her arms, her blood now in full boil.

What happened to the days when conversations respected hierarchies, recognized barriers, reflected the social order—the entirely logical, in fact, judicious, stratification on which entire civilizations had been built?

"Do I want to guess? No, I don't," and she flung her bag over her shoulder. The boy rose to his feet, gaining vertiginous height, and fixed his eyes on hers.

"I use it to pick up chicks."

"Chicks," she said, temporarily at a disadvantage.

"Chicks," he said, his eyes on her mouth once more.

There it was. There it was again—the reckless vault across generational lines, the unthinking traverse across years of hard, hard living. Somewhere in the queasy inching forward of the human species a natural restraint, a barrier built and buttressed over the generations, had vanished practically overnight with the result that children—kids barely out of high school—were holding the lives of grown women in their pale hands.

"You've been drinking, my young friend," she said. "We forgive those who drink. We forgive them everything."

The boy looked pensively at his beer. "I'm not drunk."

"No?"

"Not even close."

"You could have fooled me."

"Relax," the boy said with a slow shake of the head. "You've got to relax."

"You know," she said between tight teeth, "there is such a thing as respect. It is *owed* by the young to the old, and you don't operate outside the social protocol, my friend. You may *think* you do, but you don't. Nobody does."

The boy threw his bottle of beer in a smooth arc halfway across the kitchen into the trash can. "The social protocol?" he said. "This is America. Nobody gives a shit about the social protocol."

"Have another one," she said, turning to leave. "For the ditch."

At home she found Esperanza asleep on the couch, an empty bucket of popcorn between her legs. "Eee," she said, "I fell asleep. I never fall asleep."

"You always fall asleep. How did it go?"

"Good. You have to get her Cheetos. She says you never get her Cheetos."

"What are Cheetos?"

"Cheese puffs."

"Why would I get her cheese puffs?"

"Because she's a *kid*."

Anna had taken out her checkbook. "How much?"

"One hundred."

Anna let out a sigh. Esperanza gambled. Esperanza sat for hours on a stool, feeding coins into a slot, pulling down on a lever, cursing her fate, procuring more change, reclaiming the stool—all of it while putting away a twelve-pack of beer.

"I'll work it off. You know me, I'm a sure thing." And she was. Behind the mask of makeup, beneath the crust of jet-black hair, under the rough hoodies, the black sweats; despite the cursing, the drinking, the smoking, Esperanza was the surest thing Anna had had in a long time.

Esperanza had answered the ad for domestic help with rap music blaring in the background and had shown up at nine the following morning with fiercely minted breath and a bottle of Visine in one hand.

"People think I smoke dope because my eyes are always red," she'd said, tilting her head back and squeezing a steady stream into one eye. "But I don't. I used to. I don't anymore." So it was with understandable concern that Anna watched her go to her car, pull a vacuum cleaner out of the trunk, and come back inside as if an agreement had been made.

"And Stephanie, you know, the woman I clean rentals with? She's always, like, Espi, you have to do something about those eyes, and I'm, like, what? What can I do?" and indeed, as Anna was to find out, despite the fact that Espi *really did not smoke dope,* the crimson tide never receded, never even mellowed. By then, however, the first of many panicked calls for help had been answered, Anna's little girl punctually collected from school, brought home, fed, and put to bed at exactly eight o'clock by the only person who bothered to pick up the phone: Esperanza.

It hadn't been long before Anna met *the family*—three sisters and three brothers all living under the same roof with their errant offspring, partners, ex-partners, cousins of first, second, and third degree. Espi's stepmother, Rosa, and her father, Luis, presided over the chaos with great, if vastly tried, patience while Espi's own twenty-year-old son, christened Juan but called Thunder, went to bed content every night with a new tattoo. The door to Espi's house was always open, a pot of posole on the stove, corn tortillas warming in the oven, empty beer cans strewn liberally and abundantly in each and every room. Every month there was a christening, graduation, wedding, or burial. Anna had gone to them all.

Now, with a sigh, Anna cut the check. Esperanza tucked it expertly in her bra.

"Get her some Cheetos," she said on her way out. "Every kid should have Cheetos."

Anna crept into Eva's room, not to check on her breathing or dislodge some dark suspicion but for the pure pleasure of basking in the beauty of her sleeping child. The bridge of Eva's nose had risen slightly lately—she'd have her father's patrician beak to go with her blond hair. Settling on the edge of the bed, Anna ran a finger down her daughter's cheek.

She'd come into the world a queer bundle of reticulated flesh, her little girl, a web of capillaries running red and loud just below the skin.

"She looks like a Jackson Pollock," Anna told the nurse that first night in a hospital in Boston, where she had flown in from Africa to enjoy the privilege of a safe birth.

"Is that right?" the nurse murmured between some savage gum-chewing.

"Her capillaries," Anna said.

"Her *what,* honey?"

"Her capillaries."

"Them blood vessels you mean?"

"Blood vessels. Yes."

"What about them?"

"They're raised."

"Oh, I wouldn't worry about *that.*"

"Why not?"

The nurse, a woman with square glasses, square fingernails, and square white shoes, lifted her large, watery eyes to Anna's and let the question go unanswered. Not out of malice or intent but because she'd already forgotten it.

"I need a doctor," Anna said. "I need a doctor right now."

"What on earth for?"

"My daughter's capillaries are not normal."

"I told you, you don't need to worry about that," but Anna did worry. She raised hell until an intern from a nearby delivery showed up with a mask on his face, latex gloves on his hands. He turned the baby roughly on her back, gave a cursory look, and stormed out of the room without so much as a nod in Anna's direction.

A sound of improbable scale and depth rose out of the crib, past the hospital room, past the uninspired cheeriness of the maternity ward into the greater world where something—or nothing—was there to receive it, it was hard to tell. All Anna knew was that after the baby had been cooed, rocked, bounced, *begged* to sleep, she found herself kneeling by the bed whimpering, "Somebody help, somebody please help."

A few weeks went by before she was able to joke about Eva's peculiar range of sound. "She's a baby rights activist," or, "We have a little Maiorca in the making," but there were things that already needed hiding by then, things she'd never be prevailed upon to tell. Like the time the baby had been dropped on the couch as Anna walked in tightening circles around the living room, her hands in her hair, matching rising octave with rising octave in a surging tide of rage. Or the time she'd left Eva screaming bloody murder in the car, as she stood on the curb looking in, arms crossed against the cold, tears streaming down her face.

If motherhood leaves a residue from one lifetime to the next, a sort of encoded knowledge best deciphered at the direst times, Anna had every reason to suspect she was on round number one. Nothing had ever left her in her underwear and bra at three in the morning, screaming, "I can't do this, I can't fucking do this!" At no time in her life had she stood perfectly mute, stunned into silence by the unfathomable demand behind an infant's wail. She lived on the equator and when they returned home, she could afford a battalion of nannies; but there were things she would not delegate, especially not to the girl's father, who had excused himself from the child-rearing process at birth.

"This," he announced at a dinner party, "is the animal husbandry period, to which men are phenomenally unsuited." His only exposure to the girl was filtered through some photographic apparatus. Armed with a camera and lenses, Eva's father captured his daughter as he would a nice bit of scenery. He developed the prints, enlarged them, and glued them in oversized leather-bound albums stacked in chronological order in his study. Anna was never featured in a single photograph.

"Not one," she told her father.

"Not one?"

"Not one."

"What did you do to the poor guy? You must have done something to the poor guy."

"I didn't do anything to the guy."

"I know *you*. You did something."

"I did nothing."

Her father tapped his fingers on the table and looked away. Anna bit down on a toothpick and broke it in half.

She'd vanished for days, giving him no idea of her whereabouts. She'd tried and largely failed to hit him countless times. She'd fought a raging addiction to cocaine and lost on numerous occasions. Once, she'd called him a whore. But she'd also bought him his first flying lessons and gone over the structure and texture of clouds, the myriad manifestations of magnetism, the rate of descent after an engine failure with him before his exam. She had taken him on the road with her, she had put a meal in front of him every single night and quivered with joy at his delight, she had carried his child.

A pall of silence fell. Anna stood, gave a small shrug, and said, *"A la guerre comme à la guerre,"* but her father waved a tired hand in the air.

"This is not a war. This is a pantomime between two fools. My advice? Start taking pictures. Make sure he's not in them."

"I don't take pictures."

"Start taking pictures."

"I don't take pictures."

"Then leave him alone. He's a good father, leave him alone," and sitting at the old family table, her skin tight around her bones, bile spilling onto her tongue, Anna found herself backed up against the vast, uncluttered lath of truth.

Because it was, in fact, the truth. Eva's father had tuned in with stark curiosity—and tremulous tenderness—around the time Eva turned two and then gone on to conquer regions Anna had never even surveyed: the voice never raised, the complaint never dismissed, the extra hour spent in the service of some unsophisticated understanding, some low epiphany.

"Eva, my most precious thing, this is called a road. In the old days, this is where people walked. Today, this is where cars run. Big cars. Fast cars. Can you see them, darling?" or, "Eva, sweetheart, this is a knife. It has a handle, see? You can hold it by the handle. But this? This part is called the blade and it's sharp. It can cut you, see?" and on that occasion, with unaccountable acumen, he ran the little girl's thumb ever so slightly over the processed steel edge, leaving her with a clear sense of *sharpness* without even the intimation of a cut. Anna witnessed several similar procedures—her breath caught in her throat, her hand extended in urgent, unarticulated plea—but not once had the little girl come away injured, or even remotely troubled. The implicit threat of passing vehicles, the unsympathetic nature of sharp objects, the deep danger of edges—curbs, embankments, balconies, shores—all acquired proper significance in Eva's mind without a single yank, pull, or shout.

But that had come later, much, much later. For the longest time, for what to Anna seemed an ice age, the evolving circuitry in Eva's brain had a single, largely silent observer: her. The first months were by far the worst. At the end of a night she would remember as Hangman's Night, a cry so fractured escaped her baby's lips that Anna looked on the pale glow spreading over the garden below as if on the advance of cancer on a living body.

The cry, so disconsolate, so deep, marked a turning point in Anna's life, a moment in which absence, and not presence, laid greater claim to the marrow of things, and nothing—not the stirring of life among the leaves, not the faithful turning of the sun, not the punctual pandemonium of dawn on the equator—would ever be counted on to subvert that basic chemistry again. She'd been warned about postpartum depression, but when that implacable darkness hardened into a dumb malevolence, Anna found herself questioning the very existence of light.

She put the nannies in charge and hit the road then, returning from a magazine assignment three weeks later to a baby she barely recognized. She bounded up the stairs and ran to the crib, crushing Eva into her arms, whispering, "Mamma's back, my love, Mamma's back," only to have a howl of high-pitched protest split the night—and cleave her heart in two.

Ten days later, she was gone again. There was no breathless return this time. She climbed the stairs slowly, wondering if Eva had sprouted hair in the month she'd been away. Mother and daughter studied each other silently, Eva sitting upright by that stage, a streak of ice in her blue eyes as Anna rummaged in her bag for a tambourine-like instrument plucked out of the steaming bowels of Congo. She handed it over with a queasy smile.

"Here," she said. "Shake it." Eva closed her chubby fingers on the edge of the tambourine, held it suspiciously aloft, then brought it down with a clank onto her head. The scream that followed was operatic, nothing Anna was prepared for. Both nannies came rushing in. "What have you been feeding her?" Anna asked them before she left the room.

Funny. Funny how quickly and efficiently Anna had buried those first years, how fact had turned into pure fiction. Out of those lost latitudes, a single shard of uncontaminated evidence kept surfacing with perverse regularity: a black-and-white photograph of Eva gazing down at a cake with two candles (one for good luck) taken by her father as Anna stood in a swirl of desert dust on the roof of some abandoned building, trying to place a call.

"Why'd you bother having her?" Eva's father said when she got back. Anna pulled the vodka out of the freezer.

"I tried calling. No one picked up the phone."

16

"It was her *first* birthday for fuck's sake."

"I tried. No one answered."

Fastidious and feline in his tailored suit, Eva's father laid a coldly furious eye on her. "You were going to express your regrets to an *infant* over the phone?"

"Something like that."

"Suggesting *what,* if I may inquire, as the reason for your absence?"

"*Work,*" Anna said, knocking back a shot.

"Oh, *work,*" he said, his voice smooth and dangerous. "I'll leave you the privilege of telling her that when she's old enough." And of course, years later, when the question came out of nowhere, Anna found herself unable to meet her little girl's eyes.

"Why, Mamma?"

"I had to work."

"It was my first birthday! The biggest birthday of all!"

"Not really."

"Yes really."

"What about zero to one? Zero to one seems bigger to me."

"Mom."

"What?"

"There's no cake from zero to one."

It was impossible to explain, the obscure misery of those lost years away from her job when she was with her child, away from her child when she was on assignment, never at the right place at the right time, balanced, as if on a tightrope, between points she could never reach.

She kept it up, though, until the day a bullet came zinging past, setting off an echo in one ear. The ring became a nightly persecution, doubling in depth and strength, keeping her up, wearing her down, making her crazy in the mornings trying to light a cigarette with that dead vibration in her skull.

"Why don't you just bloody quit?" the girl's father asked, reaching over and putting out her cigarette, "You do realize you have a child."

"I thought you had one, too."

"Small children need their mothers, not their fathers."

"Says the resident expert on small children."

"I don't claim to know much about children, Anna, but what I do know, what only a fool could fail to notice, is that this constant going away on your part, this constant vanishing act, is harming her."

"How about *you* put in some time?"

"I do the best I can."

"Which, scrupulously added, comes up to *zero*. Or right around there."

"I do the best I can, Anna, the best I can. And will you please stop smoking? It's a filthy habit."

She went around to a few doctors, sat in waiting rooms with little Eva in her lap and that dead ringing in her ear, and got told the same thing over and over: avoid loud noises. So she quit her job, her life on the road, that vastness that for years had been her soul, and settled down with a man she did not trust and a toddler with an iron will. "NO," Eva had formed the habit of saying, pounding her little fist on the table. "NO."

"No?"

"NO."

"What do you mean, no?"

"NO."

"No is not an option, Eva."

"NO."

"No is the wrong answer, Eva."

"NO."

"Eva, there is no such thing as NO, do you understand?"

"NO."

Inconsistency, Anna would learn, was not one of her daughter's shortcomings. It was NO and NO and NO again until after their escape from Eva's father to a new continent, to a furnace of light at the southern end of the Rockies and to motherhood redefined, reimagined, reconceived, with Anna shuttling between therapy and parenting classes, and Eva on a stubborn diet of white bread and green beans.

"Pretty limited food range your daughter has," a mother of five astutely and perhaps not unkindly observed after a play-date.

"I know," said Anna. "I'm trying to expand it."

"She's what? Three?"

"Four."

"Too late."

"Too late to feed her?" She got a pitying look. "No. Too late to introduce her to new food."

The woman's eyes were large, her skin sufficiently translu-cent to produce in Anna an instinctive current of distrust.

"There's been research done, tons of research done, showing that infants under one will try every type of food at least *five* times if it's given to them by their mother, but *only* by their mother."

Anna looked away.

"There've been books published."

"Books?"

"Lots of books. I gave mine radishes, I gave them squash. I gave them tomatoes. And spinach. I gave them lots of spinach."

"No harm in spinach."

"I gave them sauerkraut."

"You gave them sauerkraut?"

"I gave them sauerkraut. And guess what? They *love* it."

"Right on. You've got yourself a team of sauerkraut eaters. You should field them in formation."

She got a long, cold stare; and in those large, oddly reflective eyes, as if on a screen, Anna saw herself slicing bread and boiling beans, because, just after their move, Eva would eat *nothing else*.

She tried to sneak in some whole wheat. Eva picked up the slice and held it against the light. "What's this?"

"Bread."

"Why is it dark?"

"I have no idea."

"I don't like dark bread."

"You've never tried dark bread."

"Mamma, I don't want dark bread."

"Why not?"

"Because I don't."

Motherhood multiplied by a thousand, motherhood on a constant edge, motherhood like a prison sentence until the day Anna got called in and told that her daughter was shoveling handfuls of dirt in her mouth at recess.

"Dirt?"

The teacher gave a grave nod.

"In her mouth?"

Another nod.

"She eats it?"

"We are not sure, we think she does." Nearly a minute went past before the teacher, a transplant from the Hungarian countryside raised on the milk of human kindness, took Anna's hands in hers and whispered, "Why would she do that? Why would Eva feel the need to do that?"

Reclaiming her hands with a jerk, Anna had no trouble adding up a father, a continent, two nannies, and two dogs, and saying, "She's lost everything. The girl's lost everything." A few minutes later, fumbling badly with the buckles of Eva's car seat, Anna felt her daughter's tiny palm on her cheek. "Mamma, are you crying?"

"Little bit."

"You never cry."

"No, I don't."

"Why, Mamma? Why are you crying?"

"They say you're eating dirt. They say you squat behind bushes, put dirt in your mouth and eat it."

"I can stop."

The first buckle snapped shut. "You can?"

"Yes." The second buckle slid in. "You sure?"

"It's *my* mouth, Mamma."

Things crack under too much pressure, and in the interstices occasionally new life takes root. From one day to the next, the school drop-offs, the playdates, the blessedness of Sunday mornings at home settled into a merciful routine. Eva got a dog out of a cardboard box in front of the food store and called it Paco, the Spanish nickname for Francisco. She was a bunny, a pirate, then a witch at Halloween. Anna started a column for the local paper. Eva acquired a taste for chicken and beef, zucchini and rice, shrimp tempura.

They moved houses, settling down into a narrow pass glazed with snow and ice. The roof leaked and Anna axed the ice off of it, putting in gashes a foot long. Accumulated snow snapped branches off their apple tree, tearing Anna and Eva from sleep in deep terror, and Anna pruned it at the wrong time of the year. Then frost loosened into mist, ice turned to mud, the sun rioted longer and longer over the escarpment, painting the rock beneath it all kinds of violent hues. The hummingbirds came in crazed droves. Knees against chest, Eva dropped crocus bulbs into the earth. Caught in a shaft of dying light, Anna watched.

That was how summer came that year.

Chapter Two

The sun rose over the escarpment and ran fast and hard over a stretch of broken ground on which a few casitas sat despondent, down to the river and up to the house, casting long, gaunt shadows on the patio outside. A few miles past the solitude of the mesa, past acres and acres of chamisa, past the steady metronome of what had once been a furiously blinking light, the town was starting to stir. The bells of the church of Our Lady of Guadalupe were about to resume their division of time into half-hour segments, and soon school buses would begin their artful rounds up and down dirt roads lined with *latilla* fences and red willows. Dust would rise, sounds would multiply, while all around, threaded in a near perfect circumference on the horizon, mountains solid and distant breathed out the quiet power of stone.

Anna ran both hands through her hair. Sleep had come in tight-fisted spurts, between long spells of wakefulness during which her mind had turned tirelessly around the boy. The way he'd sat loose and cool in his young body as she grew stiff in hers, the way he'd propped his elbows on the counter behind him, careless and lazy—inured, it seemed, to the standard fluttering of the human heart in the face of probable rejection.

As a rule, men approached Anna with circumspection. Those who pushed past the first exchanges nursed deep doubts, in part because of her situation—single mother, single head of household, single holder of insurance, single everything—in part because they sensed a roiling of dark particles beneath the affable exterior.

"I listen to you and you know what I hear?" one of them had taken the trouble to write in a letter posted from the middle of the American nowhere. "The hiss of a pressure cooker."

Some approaches had been more sanguine than others, but they had been on the whole discolored by doubt, tainted by fear. Anna had had a single sustained dalliance since the big move, the duration of which she could calculate in weeks rather than months. Eva had never even met him. Thinking back to the handful of seconds spent sparring with the boy, feeling the texture of her own anger as he spoke, Anna realized that what had most incensed her had been his lack of fear. But why? Why deny a boy the recklessness of youth? Why attempt, with her dismissal, to reduce his flight to a pathetic crawl? The boy was just a boy, unshackled by age and circumstance, blind to the finality of the grave, deaf to the murmurings of the dead.

Anna got up and went to the kitchen. A small voice rose from her daughter's room.

"Mamma?"

Buried beneath the covers, Eva smelled of goodness and deep sleep. Anna pulled her gently onto her lap and they stayed sitting like that for some time.

"Come on, my love, it's time for breakfast." She wrapped Eva in her polka-dotted robe, retrieved her slippers from under the bed, and together they walked to the dining room, where Eva sat waiting with ruffled hair and unfocused eyes for her bowl of cereal. At eight, the girl was old enough to get her own breakfast, but something in Anna could not, would not, give up the pleasure of feeding her own child.

When breakfast was over, Eva brought her bowl to the sink, washed it, and laid it out to dry before crossing her arms and looking around with cold, critical eyes.

"Have you packed my lunch?"

"No."

"Have you fed Paco?"

"No."

"Do I have any clean clothes?"

"In the dryer."

"Mamma."

"What?"

"You have to do a load of whites."

Anna knew legions of single mothers, agitated women at the mercy of their despotic offspring, but never had she come across a reversal of roles as clear-cut as that between Eva and herself. On the way out the door in the morning, it was Eva who emptied the trash, assembled the videos for return, made sure the dog was fed. What Anna neglected to do, Eva took care of with a roll of the eyes. "You were going to let poor Paco starve?" or, "You were going to pay *more* late fees?" Anna couldn't remember when the turnabout had taken place, when she'd gone from being at least nominally in charge to having to travel the straight and narrow all the time. All she knew is that the transition had been wonderfully smooth—a wholly implausible, yet utterly welcome, balancing of forces.

The first intimation had come one sleepy afternoon in the dead of winter when Eva, barely five, rolled out her cash register and coolly counted out one hundred eighty-two dollars and fifty-four cents. Anna had no trouble remembering her reserves at age five: they consisted strictly of IOUs, money she owed her sister, so she'd peered down incredulously. "Where'd you get that stash?"

"Some I earned, some I got given," had been Eva's arch reply. Challenged to prove it, her little girl had started accounting for every penny until, not even a quarter of the way through, Anna had begged for mercy.

The sun rose above the portal and soon it was time to run, the dog having taken position by the door at the stroke of eight, stolid and stoic in his determination not to be left behind. Eva stood by him in silence, lunch box held primly in both hands, as Anna ran cursing from room to room, looking for a book, then for the car keys, and finally for her cell phone. They ran to the truck—dog first, Eva second,

Anna third—and proceeded in a flurry of accusations and recriminations—all voiced by Eva, who hated to be late for school—past the post office and over the bridge toward town. "We'll get there on time," Anna swore, "I promise you we'll get there on time," which, barring a few exceptions, all recorded in Eva's jagged handwriting on the fridge, they never failed to do, pulling up just as Eva's classroom door inched shut.

"Did you get to school on time?" Eva's father acquired the habit of asking every time he rang.

"Kinda."

"Eva, my love, there is such a thing as an alarm clock. I am afraid it will be up to you to purchase one."

"Mamma, Daddy says we need an alarm clock," Eva said with serious eyes. After the fourth or fifth reminder, Anna grabbed the phone from her hand. "What's the endless fascination, the gnawing obsession? You want an alarm clock? Get yourself an alarm clock. Get the Swiss kind. I hear they work better."

"I have an alarm clock, Anna. It rings at precisely four-thirty in the morning."

"Get yourself another one. Maybe two will do the trick."

He put a Swiss one in the mail and Eva laid it gingerly, still unwrapped, in her room, between a framed portrait of him in high spirits and a handful of sand dollars they'd stolen together from a rising tide.

"Did you get the alarm clock I sent?" he asked the next time he called.

Eva shrugged.

"Sorry, my love, did you hear what I said?"

Filtered through wires and cables and circuit boards, not to mention land and air and dark matter both unmeasured and unclaimed, Eva's father's voice somehow rang out as if through a megaphone.

"Did you hear what I said?"

Anna began wiping down the kitchen counter.

"I put it in my room," Eva said in her small voice.

"Sorry, my love, in whose room did you put it?"

"My room."

"May I speak to your mother?"

Anna signaled wildly no.

"Mamma's in the shower."

"Darling, what's the alarm clock *doing* in your room?"

"I put it next to your picture, Daddy, and next to the sand dollars," and through silence that struck like a sandstorm, Anna heard, distinctly, the encumbered beating of the girl's heart.

"You want me to set the alarm clock?" Anna asked gently after Eva got off the phone.

"No," said Eva, and like other things—the first-aid kit Anna never got around to ordering, the educational wooden blocks she never got around to buying, the ski helmet she saw no point in spending money on—the subject was dropped, no action ever taken.

"This is the beauty of hemispheres," she told a friend whose recently divorced husband had just dropped off a drum set for their five-year-old. "They separate you from your ex."

*   *   *

Alone with the dog in the car, Anna let her forehead rest briefly on the steering wheel. Then, pushing out a long breath, she rolled down Ben Romero Road. At the highway, she took a left toward the food store.

They must have met a while back, she and the boy, before he'd gone off to college, because she'd had no trouble identifying him as Richard Strand's son the night before.

His father had come around within minutes of her arrival with skewered shrimps on a tray.

"Eat," he'd said.

"Why me?"

"Because I made them and no one's eating them."

She'd picked up a skewer. "You're going to watch me?"

"I'm thinking about it."

"Don't think. Move on. You've got a crowd to please."

Richard Strand had picked up a skewer and bitten into the impaled flesh with animal relish. "What's wrong with these fucking people?"

"They're your friends."

He'd waved a hand. "Ghosts. Mere shadows."

"Kick them out."

"I'm thinking about it."

"Call the cops."

"I'm thinking about it," and he'd moved on, turning women's heads as he went. Few men at this dry end of the Rockies dressed like Richard Strand, with a crisp linen shirt, always white, over faded jeans and soft Italian-leather shoes.

"It's obscene, the way people dress around here," she'd said to him once, not long after they met.

"I know."

"Let's all go back to the jungle. Tarzan and all that."

"You get all worked up."

"I'm not worked up."

"Why do you get all worked up?"

They'd met late one afternoon in a bowl of dust, down in the canyon, down by the river. The wind was picking things up and throwing them around with bald malevolence as Anna stood on the side of the road with her new life, her new truck, a flat tire—and no idea where the spare might be.

"You don't know where it is?"

"No."

"Meaning you might not have one."

"Possibly."

"You're driving around without a spare tire."

"No, not necessarily. I'm assuming there's one somewhere."

"But you don't know where."

"No."

Then by chance she had moved right next door to Richard Strand, on the same side of the Rio Hondo, which ran cold and fast into the Rio Grande and there crashed and bled—thinned out, forgotten—to the Mexican border. Richard Strand's house was bigger than hers. It was full of flowers, full of birds in small cages, fish in aquariums, walls with memories twenty years thick, children's laughter somewhere in the back, so she had quickly formed the habit of going over.

Richard Strand was a man without prejudices, a quality never more apparent than when he spoke to his youngest children—Matthew and Mickey, respectively nine and six—to whom he would say, "You're right, buddy, they suck! Sharp corners suck! What are we going to do about this one you keep hitting your head on?" Or, "I couldn't agree with you more, bud, it's a hot oven, a really hot oven, I'm not surprised your hand hurts." And once, sensationally, "I know, buddy, I know. Who put these steps here? That's what I want to know. Who put these steps here?"

But Richard Strand was also a man of fixed emotions. Anna had never seen him angry or upset, she'd never heard him swear or raise his voice. Despite the cinematic, almost hypnotic appearance of various girlfriends in various getups, Richard's house had become the closest thing to a sanctuary Anna could think of.

"It's like you're a private signatory to the Geneva Convention," she'd said with feeling once, seconds before a girl barely out of high school streaked across the living room screaming, *"Chinga la puta de tu madre!"* and slammed the front door behind her. Richard had let out a sigh.

"You pick them too young."

"I know."

"Why do you pick them so young?"

"I don't know."

"Stop picking them so young."

*   *   *

The parking lot of the food store was full, which put the estimated shopping time for a gallon of milk and a dozen eggs at roughly half an hour. There were going to be the mothers, a clear-eyed, hard-calved army in Birkenstocks and socks, a few fathers, many with the lowered stares of the routinely prevailed upon, a few casual acquaintances in need of a good confession, someone from her yoga studio eager to discuss her back bends. It was going to take a lifetime just getting to the checkout line. Sighing, Anna went in.

She charged head down through the aisles, making it to the refrigerated food section without a hitch. She descended like a bird of prey on the milk, pressed a carton of eggs to her chest, turned, mentally homed in on the shortest line to the nearest register, and there—doll-like, beautiful, eyes like fields of cannabis swaying gently in the wind—was Ree.

"What are you doing here?" Ree asked.

"I'm buying food."

"It's a food store, Anna. What else would you be buying?"

"I agree. What else would I be buying?"

"I mean now, this early in the morning."

"I'm always in here this early in the morning."

"You are? How come I never see you?"

"Because you're always stoned."

"I'm stoned now and you're in perfect focus."

"I don't know, it's a good question. You want to talk about it?"

32

"Not really. Just tell me how you are."

A woman was advancing down the aisle with two children like ripe plums, like sweet candy in her cart, and Anna could not help a smile. Increasingly, children were becoming the only thing worth looking at. Like the silver veins of rivers and oceans, the raw flanks of mountains, they had the power to leave her mute.

"How am I? Let's see. I had this kid, this *child,* come on to me last night."

Behind a fog of dope, Ree's eyes remained perfectly motionless.

"Age of consent?"

"Jesus, Ree."

"What do you mean, Jesus? You never know with these things, they creep up on you. Anyway. What was I saying?"

"Age of consent."

"Right. How did you meet?"

Her eyes on the children, Anna shook her head. "I don't remember," she said. "I don't remember how we met."

It could only have been years before, when the boy had been too young to make an impression. She had a fairly sturdy recollection of the boy's entirely unexpected acceptance into an Ivy League school because Richard wouldn't shut up about the money.

"I could buy a house, I could own real estate in Florida."

"Don't send him."

"The room deposit? A thousand bucks."

"He doesn't need to go."

"The textbooks? Two grand."

"Keep him home. Have him polish your shoes. It's a dying art."

"Tuition? Don't get me started on tuition."

"He could set up a stand at Grand Central Station."

"People *live* on that kind of money. They *live* on it."

"Or Penn Station. There's always Penn Station."

He'd pushed her out the door with the excuse that his youngest son, Mickey, had tripped and hit his head. "I know, bud," she heard him say as the door closed shut. "It's that table. How about we get rid of that table? You and me, huh?"

But that was all. That was all she could remember.

Anna parked, crossed S. Street, feeling, as she did, the hard mineral aggregate of the high desert on her tongue and wondering for the millionth time why she, who loved water so much, had settled on such badly broken ground. There was a town in the state called No Agua. It wasn't that far away.

She inspected the row of names on the buzzer, pushed the one that said Dr. Roemer, climbed one flight of stairs to the waiting room, picked up a magazine, beheld a woman's naked buttocks for a split second, then let her eyes drift to the window—to a tree shooting up like a tongue of silver fire against the unfiltered blue of the New Mexican sky. "Relax," the boy had said with the authority conferred by zero obligations, zero deadlines, a handful of bonds—and then only of the lightest fabric.

"I slept like shit," she told Dr. Roemer before even sitting down. The doctor's face was like a slab of stone.

"You always sleep like shit."

"Which is my curse, my cross to bear, but last night was worse."

"Why was it worse?"

"I met a boy."

"Whose boy?"

"You mean whose son?"

The doctor, a man bovine in mass and apparent temperament, gave her a slow nod.

"My neighbor's son," she said. "Friend and neighbor, actually. Good friend, stellar neighbor. Waters my plants when I'm away."

"Does he know?"

"What?"

"That you're sleeping with his son."

"Who's sleeping with his son? I'm not sleeping with his son. You think terrible things about me. All the time you think terrible things. Like I don't pay you. Like I walk away without paying you."

"Why did you sleep like shit then?"

"Because I kept thinking about my neighbor's son, which is different from sleeping with my neighbor's son. It's a comparatively innocuous occupation, you must admit."

"But you couldn't stop."

"Stop what?"

"Thinking about him."

"No."

"Why not?"

"Let's see. Chemistry. Physical attraction. My body. His body. You know."

"His body wasn't in your room last night. It's not in this room today."

Anna cocked her head.

"Excuse me?"

"His body is not in this room."

"So?"

"So what are you attracted to?"

Anna let her eyes wander. "I'm weary of your traps, Doctor Roemer, so I'll tentatively, very tentatively, say the idea of his body."

"That's right. An idea that lives in your mind, which is the same thing as a story you're telling yourself: I need this boy's body to be happy."

"Who's talking about happiness? This is sex at its most basic."

"Fine, let's try a little variation. I need sex with this boy to be happy. Is that true?"

"It's not untrue."

"So you have sex. Because of the nature of your attraction, you keep having sex. Then you start wanting things a . . . how old is he?"

"Twenty. Maybe twenty-one."

"Okay. You start wanting things a twenty-year-old can't give you and he starts wanting things a forty-year-old can't give him, and what happens next?"

"Train wreck."

The doctor smiled. "So let's do this one more time. I need sex with this boy to be happy. Is that true?"

"No."

"And if that's not true, *what is?*"

For a while neither of them spoke.

"I don't know," Anna said. "I don't know what's true."

The doctor clapped a soundless clap. "In China they say, live in a state of constant unknowingness."

"We're not in China."

"China, not China, it's all the same. If you were prepared to live in a state of constant unknowingness, you would not be sleeping like shit."

"Maybe I should move to China."

"Maybe."

"You got a place in China?"

"No."

"That's crazy. You'd think you'd have a castle by now, a place with a pool at the very minimum."

"I've never been to China. Have you ever not paid me?"

"Never."

"Good. You got me worried."

"I start today. On account of all the bullshit you've been giving me without a fixed domicile in China."

"Anna."

"What?"

"Leave the kid alone."

"Why?"

"He's fixing to fuck you up real good."

Chapter Three

Summer ripened slowly. First the ground hardened, next the wind died and the sage, dormant throughout spring, came to life with a whisper and a smell to it. Anna took Eva and Paco to the river every day, and the two took turns jumping in and out with sticks in their mouths.

The great river. The strong river of the north. Anna had looked it up when she first moved. To the Apaches it was *Kotsoi,* the Great Waters. For the Tewas it was *Posoge,* the Big River. Only the Navajos, the vanquished lords of what was once a nation, called it something else entirely. To them it was the *Tooh Ba'aadii,* the Female River, because it flowed south, a feminine direction, and no name seemed to Anna more intuitively attuned to the nature of a waterway that cuts canyons, threads basins, finds its way to the sea, with barely a whisper.

At the water's edge, the earth behind them dreamed itself

into root and bark. Anna offered her face to the sun and gave silent thanks. The tempest raised by the boy had passed, almost forgotten now. She'd run into Richard Strand at the food store one afternoon.

"Come to dinner," he said.

"Who's coming?"

He waved a casual hand. "Kids, a couple pals, the usual. I haven't seen you in a while."

She looked around her. "We're always here. How come we're always here?"

Richard Strand had considered the question neutrally. "We're buying food."

"I know. But it's like we're enslaved. We're always here, with our little carts, running into each other, buying food."

"You get all worked up. Why do you get all worked up?"

"I'm not worked up."

"Come for dinner."

"No."

Richard Strand's eyebrows had shot up.

"No?"

"No."

"Why not?"

"I've got a friend in the hospital." And she'd taken off, leaving Richard Strand standing, jaw a little slack, in the cheese section.

Since then, life had lost its sting. Esperanza's transmission had died a sudden death and Anna had gone around to the shop. "Three thousand dollars," she'd told Esperanza that evening, handing her the bill. Esperanza had slapped a hand on her mouth.

"*Ohi, mi madre!*"

"*Ohi, mi madre* is right," Anna had said; and so for now, until Esperanza worked off her debt, there were three of them in the house: Anna in her study pushing words around the junkyard of her mind, Esperanza and Eva eating popcorn on the couch.

The two were thick as thieves. "Mom," Eva called out the day Esperanza moved in, "you need to get Espi Jenny Craig!"

In her study, Anna pressed save on her computer once more.

"What's Jenny Craig?"

"Diet meals!" Esperanza shouted. "It's how Mary Martinez got skinny! She was big, no? And now she's wearing skinny jeans!"

"You owe me three thousand bucks, Esperanza."

"But I'm here, no? I'm working!"

"Three thousand, Espi."

"Eee, your mother is hard, but I'm a sure thing, right, Eva? I'm a sure thing," and Eva, whose wrists were like popsicle sticks, yelled out, "I want Jenny Craig, too!"

At her desk a few days later, in the same agony of silence, of failure, of new and old beginnings, Anna saw Esperanza's head pop in through the opened door. "We're going to Sonic."

"What's Sonic?"

"The slushy place!" a small voice shouted from behind the door. "No slushes," Anna said, and a couple hours later there was half a Frito pie and two empty bucketfuls of orange slush in the trash.

None of it, however expertly orchestrated, prevented Espi from getting it in the neck.

"Espi."

"Yes, *mijita.*"

"Your eyes are always red."

"Eee, I know! What can I do? I don't know what to do! I'm always putting this stuff in!" And Esperanza pulled out a bottle of maximum-strength Visine—pure bleach by the look of it—and waved it in the air with clear animosity. "And it's expensive! Five dollars a bottle. Six with tax! And it lasts me a week!"

"Espi?"

"Yes?"

"Why are your eyes always red?"

"Don't ask me! Ask my mother! It's how I was born!"

"You were born with red eyes?"

Espi, whose crimson sclera were the result of prodigious beer drinking after Eva went to bed, cast a furtive glance in Anna's direction.

"Eva, go do your homework."

"I don't have any homework."

"Go do something."

"Like what?"

"Go run around outside. Take Paco with you."

"Paco's tired," Eva said as the Lab, having perceived a summons and sensed the possibility of some retrieving, stood salivating by her leg.

"Paco is not tired. Paco is dying to go."

Eva took Paco's head in her small hands. "You're tired, aren't you? Aren't you, Paco?" and the dog, spiritually attuned to the child in a way Anna had always found miraculous, lay down and let his head rest on her feet.

Down by the river, afternoons, she and Eva played games. Eva put a fishnet bag over Paco's head and they took bets on how long it would take him to paw it off. The dog became a regular Houdini, extricating himself with increasing economy of movement in preparation for some great vanishing act that would teach them both a lesson.

In the falling light, as the river went from silver to jade, they wrote words on each other's backs and had to guess. Looking at a book, they tightened knots along a piece of rope, undid them, learned how they went from memory over and over again. On an old tree trunk, feet off the ground, Eva was the captain, Anna the sailor.

"'O Captain! my Captain!' Where to?"

"The Galapagos! Barbados! Neptune! Jupiter! Orion!"

And next, Anna would intone, "'I've seen things you people wouldn't believe. Warships on fire off the shoulder of Orion...'" and Eva, who had never seen *Blade Runner* but had memorized the speech, would almost always cut in.

"Mamma."

"What?"

"It's 'attack ships,' not 'warships.'"

43

"'Attack ships on fire off the shoulder of Orion. I watched b-beams shine in the dark near the Tannhäuser Gate . . .'"

"Mamma."

"What?"

"It's 'c-beams,' not 'b-beams.'"

"Since when?"

"Since the movie."

"'I watched c-beams shine . . .'"

"It's 'glitter.' Not 'shine.'"

They unraveled time, simply by lying there, under the great sky.

"What's your first memory?" Eva asked one day as a pale quarter moon rose over the canyon.

"I don't know."

"Everyone has a first memory."

"I don't know."

"Mamma."

"I'm serious, I don't know. What's yours?"

"You covered in blood. And dust. You covered in blood and dust."

On this cracked land at the northern end of the desert, much had been forgotten, much cast aside. Anna propped herself on her elbows, jolted into memory. It seemed like another life, the day she'd climbed barefoot and drunk on a dirt bike in the African bush and set out, cursing, for something she had no chance of finding—not in the cold, cold shadow of Eva's father. Hours later, when she'd finally found her way back, shaking from the trauma of a fractured shoulder and badly lacerated skin, he had looked her over and picked up the car keys on his way out. He'd resurfaced three days later.

"Get out," she'd said.

"I told you not to get on that bike."

"I said, get out."

"I told you."

"What are you after? A prize for telling me?"

"I can't do this anymore."

"Nobody is asking you to."

"Anna."

"Nobody's asking you shit."

Now, behind mother and daughter, the river flowed thick and slow to the Mexican border. Walls of basalt rose on either side, intricately cracked, split deep from top to bottom.

"Where were you?" asked Anna.

"At the door when you came in."

"With Lynette?"

"Yes."

"I didn't see you."

"It's okay."

"I'm so sorry."

"It's okay."

"No it's not okay. It's fucked up."

"Mamma."

"What?"

"You have to stop swearing."

*   *   *

Back at home, Esperanza had the cleaning channel on and a list, queasily committed to paper, of wipes and mops and degreasers and polishes Anna had to get for her at the store the next day. Anna made dinner, and in the simple lowering of food to the table, in the plain offering of victuals, found unimaginable release, a stillness close to peace. Esperanza poked at her zucchini, ignored all lettuce, grew faint at the sight of chard, and typically lasted no more than half an hour before heading out to Sonic.

"I want to go with Espi!" Eva screamed when Espi got up from the table.

"Eat your dinner."

"But I want to go with Espi!"

Esperanza had one foot out the door—cigarette dangling off the corner of her mouth, lighter held aloft already. "Do what your mother tells you," she said.

"But I want a slushy!"

"Do what your mother tells you," Esperanza said and pulled the door shut.

That night, in bed, Eva added a third prayer to her list.

"Dear God and all the angels," she said, holding her mother's hand in hers. "Please help Mamma not to swear."

When Esperanza came back, three hours later, she stank of booze and cigarette smoke. She gestured Anna to the door.

"Is Eva in bed?"

"She is," said Anna.

"Good. I don't want her seeing me like this."

*   *   *

It was summer. Things were fast forgotten, soon forgiven. Esperanza instructed Eva in the art of cop interception through some listening device purchased from a drug dealer in Espanola and strove to impress upon them both the futility of geometry.

"What is she going to do with the area of a square when she grows up?"

"Espi," said Eva, looking up from her math workbook.

"Yes, *mijita?*"

"It's a rhombus."

"Eee, that's even worse! They should be teaching her how to make money on that thing in New York, no? What's it called, Anna, that thing in New York?"

"The Stock Exchange."

"The Stock Exchange. So she doesn't end up like me, living in someone's house, mopping their floors, doing their laundry, because she can't afford a transmission, no?"

"Espi," Eva said, peering up out of grave eyes. "The reason you never have any money is because you gamble."

Esperanza picked up a rag and shook it out. *"Hija,"* she said, "I have never gambled in my life."

Eva approached her mother obliquely a few days later in the kitchen, clearly intending to part with a piece of information of some significance. "Mamma," she whispered, "Espi has a Taser! A pink Taser!"

"Why does Espi have a Taser?"

47

"I don't know!" said Eva, her eyes cutting about the room.

"Esperanza," said Anna that night over dinner, "why do you have a Taser?"

"Eee!" said Esperanza. "Because you never know!"

"Never know what?"

"Who could be there!"

"There where?"

"Anywhere!" Esperanza said, getting up with her plate. She only approached Anna after the girl had fallen asleep. "I got it for Eva," she whispered, "for when she turns nine."

It was summer, there were no more mad dashes out the door in the morning, no shrill recriminations with the dog cowering in the back of the truck. Time softened, lengthened, grew more lenient. Eva sat her mother down at the dinner table with paper and pencil. "Do you remember the old house when we had to build the fence for Paco?"

Anna nodded, thankful those days were gone. She'd turned into a taxi service then, taking phone calls at all hours of the day and night from people whose greeting was, "Hi, you don't know me but I have your dog . . ." She'd shown up at various residences with smoke coming out of her ears, determined to give the dog a beating, only to have him greet her with such wild abandon she lowered the tailgate of her truck without a word of censure and watched him leap, a great smile on his face, onto the back of the truck and, there, resume position as unrewarded navigator. She had picked a house with a fenced

48

yard after that, and the dog, nicknamed by those who knew him The Forlorn Paquito, became even more forlorn.

"Yes, I remember perfectly."

"You remember the fence?"

"No."

"It was made of metal."

"I remember metal."

"It's what we're going to get for the chickens."

"What chickens?"

"The chickens we're going to get."

The difference between them: Anna had never felt the slightest connection to the ground, not once had she experienced the urge to sink something into it and watch it grow. The mere idea of chickens made her queasy; the duty of recycling or, God forbid, composting, was one that belonged to others, yet her daughter had directed countless campaigns for a vegetable garden, had commandeered their vehicle repeatedly to the recycling plant, and had emerged from various chicken coops owned by friends holding not one, not two, but *three* sharp-beaked, crazy-eyed things lovingly in her arms, as if they were puppies.

"Chickens stink," Anna said.

"But Mamma . . ."

"They stink," Anna said.

Summer carries with it both mutiny and slumber. The heat swallows hours, entire midsections of the day, but beneath all that something always stirs, something always pulls, a kind of anarchy just below the skin, something to do with the body—what the body might want, what the body might get, should the heat hold.

On one end of town, not far from an abandoned mill, a marquee went up for the Croquet Party, a seasonal extravaganza sponsored by a few good families on a single premise: that everyone wear white. Eva agreed to a white T-shirt over white tennis shorts. After standing in front of the closet for a long time, Anna pulled out a short thing with a zipper down the back.

Ree called. "What are you wearing?"

"A short dress."

"How short?"

"Roughly ten centimeters above the knee."

"I don't do centimeters."

"I don't do inches."

"Does it cover your ass?"

"Vaguely."

"Remain standing. Defy gravity and remain standing," which Anna did, in exactly the same spot, with a great many people swirling around until the crowd parted along some preordained diagonal and Richard Strand approached, son in tow.

"Anna," Richard said, leaning in for a kiss, "you remember my son Jack." And before she could take up arms, before she could *conceive* of a defense, never mind raise one, Anna felt something turn in the middle of her—a slow movement just below the heart.

"Of course," she said, trading a casual nod for a burning stare.

"She's jumped ship," Richard Strand told his son. "I haven't seen her since the *mojito* party."

"She's been keeping the hell away," said the boy.

"She's been keeping the hell away?" Richard Strand inquired mildly. His son nodded.

"You've been keeping the hell away?" asked Richard.

"Me?" said Anna, her eyes on the shimmering crowd, a ghost of a smile on her lips.

"Yes, you," said the boy.

She fixed him with cold eyes. "Richard," she said, "this is the second time your son has forgotten his manners."

Richard Strand turned to his son. "You've been disrespectful?"

The boy shrugged. "I don't know. What's disrespectful?"

"There are very clear standards," said Anna. "Very, very clear standards."

"Show them to me," said the boy.

"There are rules," Anna snapped. "Rules of conduct, rules of behavior. There is a stratified order from which *you* are not exempt."

"A what?"

"A stratified order."

Richard Strand laid a hand on the boy's shoulder. "Son, answer the question. Have you been disrespectful?"

"Depends."

"On what?"

"On what she wants," and for some reason, in the tempest of blood raised by the son, it was to the father Anna turned.

"You've got a problem," she said. "A very big problem."

Richard Strand looked at her out of clear eyes. "My son has never been a problem," he said, so after a moment of clerical silence, Anna left them both standing under the marquee muttering, "motherfucker," as she went.

The boy was everywhere that night, everywhere she looked, everywhere she turned, curse and apparition, apparition and curse, shoulders broad and loose beneath his T-shirt, hips fine and narrow in his jeans. Anna called on the moon repeatedly for help, a low, lazy moon in the lowest quadrant of the sky at first; a hard, distant globe glaring down on human folly by the end. Tight in her skin, hot in her head, she resolved a thousand times to leave but didn't. Every time she looked up, he was there, his eyes fixed knowingly on hers.

It was infuriating. The boy's relationship to the ground was so smooth, the core of him so casually aligned with the visible and invisible worlds, that Anna felt compelled to revisit her youth: had she ever stood that way? Unlikely. But it wasn't just that. The boy did not just stand with full possession of his body, he stood with full awareness of the magnetic pull of his body. Time and again she battled the urge to go over and teach him a lesson but turned her back on him instead as the moon leveraged itself higher and higher in the sky.

At one point, blurred, indistinct, Anna went inside searching for the bathroom, thinking not of the boy but of Richard Strand, of the love he had for his children. Destiny had been cruel, denying the man full custody through three divorces, but now this son, the first of five, was here to stay. She pulled her dress down, opened the door, stepped out in the hallway, and came to a sudden stop. There, his clear eyes on hers, was the boy.

Nothing was said, not a word exchanged. He covered the distance between them, laid his hands on her hips and pressed her slowly against the wall.

She had no idea how long it was before they heard some shuffling, a muffled exchange followed by an indignant, "Mom!" She disengaged to find Eva and two newly acquired minions—one of whom had his mouth screwed in an expression of infinite disgust—gaping up at her. "Go!" she said, but her daughter pointed a stiff accusatory finger at her and shouted, "You're kissing him! Stop kissing him!"

"Go!" she said again. "I'll be right out!" Eva stormed out, miniature slaves in tow, but Anna stayed right where she was, doing the exact same thing, until the weight of it started to bear down on her and she pulled away.

"Stop it!" she hissed.

The boy grabbed a fistful of hair and lowered his mouth to hers. "You stop it."

It took a second, organized revolt by her daughter for them to finally part. Anna's first, searing recollection the morning after was her own child marching her imperiously away as people exchanged amused looks.

The phone had rung the minute they got home.

"Hello," had whispered Anna, still unstable on her feet.

"Oh, you're home. How unexpected. May I speak to my daughter?"

"What time is it?" she'd asked.

"I haven't got the faintest. Not in your part of the world anyway. May I speak to my daughter?"

"What time is it where you are? I mean, it's like, what, four o'clock in the morning?"

"I have a mother, Anna, thank you, I'm sure she's in bed right now. May I speak to my daughter?"

"I mean it, what are you doing up so late?"

"I am not in England, Anna."

"No? Where are you?"

"Where I am should hardly concern you considering you chose to take up residence on some scrap of barren land on the other side of the world."

"It's not the other side of the world."

"It is *precisely* the other side of the world. Measure it. May I speak to my daughter?"

"Eva," said Anna with a sigh. "Your father is on the phone."

Breakfast was a tricky affair. Sensing the mood, Esperanza lit a cigarette and left. Mother and daughter sat across the table in silence until Anna said, with some determination, "I didn't do anything wrong."

"You were kissing him!"

"So what? He's not married, I'm not married, where's the problem?"

"Mom! You don't kiss boys at parties!"

"You don't kiss boys at parties? The whole reason you *go* to parties, the whole reason parties were invented, is to kiss boys at parties. You don't kiss boys at parties. That's the craziest thing I've ever heard in my life."

Eva rolled her eyes. "Mom."

"What?"

"It's like me going out with a *four*-year-old."

"Four and a half."

"Mom."

"Jesus, Eva, what?"

"I don't want that boy coming over."

"Coming over? Who said he was coming over?"

Eva let her spoon slide into the milk and tucked her small hands between her knees so Anna went around to her side of the table and whispered, "It's okay, my love, I promise you he won't come over."

Eva raised her moon-eyes to hers. "Pinky promise?"

Anna curled her pinky around her daughter's. "Pinky promise."

Chapter Four

Nights passed on currents of such violent longing that Anna set to work keeping thoughts and memories at bay. She purchased new and old fiction, new and old nonfiction. She read about the Mongols, the rise and fall of the Duke of Zhou. She bought yarn and made Eva a cap that fit her so well she was compelled to make another for Paco, with holes for his ears. She downloaded a chess program and spent hours getting her ass kicked by her computer, whose advertised neutrality she began to doubt.

"Mom, how can you hate a machine?"

"There's something in there, I know there's something in there."

Esperanza leaned in to get a closer look. "Where?"

"Under the keyboard."

"Let's take it apart," said Eva, and Esperanza, whose clan had produced some legendary *brujas*—witches who laid waste to lives and pastures with simple incantations—jumped back and said, "*Hija*, there are things we do not play with."

Time passed. Anna ran into Richard Strand at the food store. He asked her what was wrong. "I never see you anymore."

"I've got a million things."

"Like what?"

"A friend in the hospital."

"Another one?"

"Same one."

"Is it my son?" he asked.

Anna gave a vehement shake of her head.

"Then what?"

"Nothing. Come over. This afternoon. Bring Matthew and Mickey."

His eyes lit up at the offer, and later that day he covered the fifty yards between them and sat with her talking about debts owed and never paid, partnerships run aground, the new sushi place in town, until a scream broke the peace and they rushed outside to find Mickey on his back, underneath the apple tree. The kid was fine, his father wasn't.

"That's one hell of a dangerous tree you've got there, Anna."

"Dangerous? What's dangerous about it?"

"It's *big*. Isn't that right, buddy? Isn't that a big tree?"

"Richard."

"What?"

"A tree is a tree."

"Baloney," he said.

"Baloney?"

"Baloney."

Another week went by. Esperanza was arrested for disorderly conduct in one of the casinos, and Anna bailed her out at four o'clock in the morning.

"Don't tell Eva," were Espi's first words. "Swear to God you won't tell Eva," but of course at the breakfast table Eva sat up in her pajamas. "Oh my God!" she shrieked. "What happened to you?"

"Nothing."

"Mom, she's got a black eye! Espi's got a black eye!"

Anna stood over her with a bowl of cereal. "It's okay," she said. "She's predisposed."

"Espi, I want to know what happened."

Esperanza reached instinctively for her cigarettes. "*Mijita…*" she said.

"No *mijita*. Tell me what happened," and bit by bit, as Anna presided queasily over the improbable exchange between a child and a *norte mexicana* with the entire history of her dry land—the cellular awareness of so much spilled blood—scored in her face, the story came out of how a man had said something he shouldn't have.

"Why did you have to hit him? Why couldn't you just walk away?"

Esperanza and Anna exchanged a brief look. Underneath it all, the two women spoke the same dialect, they were equally versed in the language of violence, equally incapable of brooking or even understanding the type of compromise that seemed to come so naturally to Eva.

"What do you mean, why did she have to hit him? He *asked* for it," said Anna.

"You don't go around hitting people," said Eva.

Silence fell like a gavel.

"Mamma?"

"Yes."

"You gave me too much cereal."

Later that day the phone rang with a number no one recognized, and Anna backed away from it as if from fire. "Hey," the message said. "This is my number. Call me."

"This is my number. Call me. What's that? How do you begin to account for that?"

"Eee," Esperanza said. "That's nothing."

"Nothing? I could be his mother."

"Wait until he takes you out to dinner and he has no gas to get back home, forget picking up the check. I need rubbing alcohol."

"Why?"

"I want to mix it with Windex."

"Why do you want to mix it with Windex?"

"So it doesn't streak. I saw it on the cleaning channel."

Anna set out toward town with the dog in the back. To her right, a horse corral was decaying placidly under the great sky. To the left, the untrammeled earth rose and fell great distances along lines both jagged and smooth all the way to the horizon.

The sagebrush swayed on either side of her, pliant and docile and nearly gray among so much gray rock.

Anna thought of a conversation she'd had shortly before the big move, a quiet exchange with an old friend in which she had coolly, dispassionately stated, "A place is just a place." She'd picked New Mexico for no other reason than she'd been told it was cheap and cheerful, yet after they arrived—she and her little girl with their overnight bags full of all the wrong things—Anna had stepped out into the vastness with a cup of coffee and this place, this uncontained earth under this uncontained sky, had become as necessary to her as the air she breathed.

It hadn't been easy. She wasn't a parking lot mom, not a member of that colorful congregation of formidable hikers who somehow found the time to linger at drop-off and pickup, having formed, Anna suspected, fast friendships in the midwifery center in town. She did not escort her daughter to her classroom by the hand, as seemed to be the custom in the morning, nor did she loiter in the playground waiting for the children's collective disposition to mature into a staggered, orderly departure from the sandbox or the swings. She had stopped counting hoarsely to ten, more for Eva's sake than for that of a curiously attired mother of three who had approached her—red-faced, a strange tic in one eye—and informed her that counting to ten had come to constitute verbal and emotional abuse.

"We do not count to ten," the woman said.

"You don't count to ten."

"Absolutely not."

"What do you do?"

"We wait."

"You wait for *them?*"

"Exactly."

"For the children?"

"For the children."

"You, the grown-ups, wait for the children."

"That's correct."

"You should stop smoking dope."

"I don't smoke dope."

"You're smoking too much dope."

It had taken some convincing—a few deliberately repetitive talks on the ills of wasting time with no time to waste—but Eva had eventually formed the habit of detaching herself from play the second her mother materialized at the far edges of the playground, reducing Anna's commerce with the other mothers to zero, and multiplying their dislike of her by a thousand. She had taken no notice until the May Fair, when she'd run into a wall of hostility so thick that she had left Eva with Ree and hightailed it.

"I don't understand," she said to Ree that evening. "What have I done?"

"You don't mingle. You don't volunteer."

"I don't have *the time* to mingle. I don't have the time to volunteer!" and to a measurable extent, that was true. After several glorious months of self-financed unemployment, Anna had gotten a job cooking, initially just a couple prep shifts dicing onions and making mayonnaise, then, thanks to the high volatility of all restaurant kitchens, full exposure to the hissing, blistering, humbling inferno of the line.

"You don't have time? Well, guess what? Neither do they. They *make the time,* they make the effort."

"But why?"

"Because a school, every school, is a community project."

"A community project? What are you talking about? I'm paying trained professionals to give my daughter an education. Isn't that enough?"

"Start volunteering," Ree said.

Anna remembered signing off with high amusement on the promise to contribute thirty-five hours of volunteer work to the school. The day after the May Fair, Clean-Up Day, she'd shown up with her own vacuum cleaner, as per instructions, and vacuumed the hell out of every room. The following day, a Monday, she had sent Eva back to the swings.

"Nice day," she'd said to one of the mothers, and while that first approach had gone entirely unrewarded, others hadn't. Slowly, purely through the forgiveness built into the matrix of every woman with small children, she had found her place.

At the old blinking light, Anna put the car into neutral, checked her phone for reception, saw something out of the corner of one eye, and turned to catch the boy streaking past

her like an arrow shot by a jealous god. Off the seat, beau-
tifully balanced on the pedals of his mountain bike—shirt
unbuttoned, body offered recklessly to the sun—he saw her
and he hit the brakes, coming to an abrupt stop as she drove
past.

She crossed the intersection and a few minutes later found
herself parked outside the grocery store in a world flattened to
the single dimension of Richard Strand's son. She dialed Ree's
number.

"The boy was on a bike," she said.

"A bike?"

"A bike."

"Like, a bicycle?"

"Yeah, a bicycle."

"Is that good or bad?"

"The boy is ambulating. The boy should stay home."

"Have him arrested."

"The boy should remain *indoors*."

"Have him shot. No, wait, shoot him yourself. Go to Wal-
mart, get a gun, and shoot him."

Anna took out her car key and ran it hard and fast into the
cool metal of a post. "I've done everything right, Ree. I've behaved impeccably. I'm minding my own business, I'm driving
across town, and suddenly, there he is. On a *bike*."

"I'm telling you, shoot the motherfucker. That way he won't
be riding his bike no more."

Anna hung up, checked her watch, and called Mia, who was
never home.

"I saw him," she told the machine. "He had his shirt undone, flapping behind him in the wind. What happened to decency? What happened to the social protocol? Since when do people get to ride around with their shirts undone? And you're never home. You realize you're never home?"

It was hours before she could begin to see that Dr. Roemer was right, that it was all in her mind. Out of her fevered fantasy, out of her endlessly turning mind, had come a projection of need so strong she had galloped to the kitchen less than a week before, grabbed a piece of paper, and written in breathless, jagged strokes, *I want you so much my mouth hurts.* Had her mouth really hurt? It was hard to tell but it was easy to see, as she rolled up to the old blinking light on her way back, the arbitrary creation of the arbitrary need.

At the light she covered her face with both hands, appalled by the morning's violent spasm. A boy flying past on a bike belonged to the world and to godlike the laughter of children through the leaves, the tumult of water over stone, the languor of summer. Let the boy ride his bike, thought Anna, let the boy go; and suddenly, for the first time in weeks, she felt her soul grow still and expand into a state of measurable freedom.

She drove the rest of the way home whistling badly out of tune, stopped by the post office, picked up a stack of bills, and covered the short distance to her house. There, propped against her gate, was a bicycle. A gray bicycle slashed through with red, a pedal still slowly turning.

Anna got out and stared, silence settling like dust over the bicycle, the dirt road behind her, the house before her, and every little thing in between: the weeds pushing blindly through flagstone and gravel, the undecipherable progress of a beetle on the gate, the acrobatics of two white butterflies engaged in play. Heart pounding, she pushed the gate open.

He was sitting bare-chested on the step by her front door, elbows propped on knees, chin propped on hands. "What are you doing without a shirt on?" Anna said, her voice strange to her own ears.

The boy stood up, sinewy and muscular at once, strong and pale and loose, his veins cutting languidly down the length of his long arms, a tattooed dragon brooding darkly over one shoulder.

"Let's go," she said. "Let's get that shirt back on."

He slid a lazy hand into the pocket of his jeans. "Why?"

"What do you mean, why? You're on my property. You're not wearing a shirt. People wear shirts when they are on my property. People wear shirts in *general* when they are in public."

The boy spread his arms to encompass his surroundings. "You call this public? It's fenced."

"I'm not about to debate public and private with you. Put that shirt back on."

Lips compressed around a little smile, the boy picked up a balled shirt off the ground, snapped it open, and pulled it on as Anna began to shout, "Esperanza? Eva?"

"No one's home," the boy said, and before Anna could process the anomaly, he reached for the grocery bag.

"Let me give you a hand."

"What hand? Get off my porch."

"Jesus Christ. What are you so scared of?"

"Who's scared? I'm not scared. Get off my porch."

"I'm not getting off your fucking porch!"

Anna pulled out her house keys and dangled them in the air.

"I'm going to go inside. As a favor to your father, I'm going to put these things in the fridge and count to ten before I call the cops."

She had the phone in one hand, she had her thumb on the number nine, she had her line ready. *There is a young intruder on my property, he's unarmed and seemingly well-intentioned but refuses to leave.* She had the first stirrings of melancholy already, the cold crash of chemicals after a sudden spike. She had cold skin and a cold heart, both feet in the grave and only going through the motions, when the boy, her neighbor's son, stepped coolly inside and flowed nearly undetected through time and circumstance, gliding as if on wheels across the living room to the window where she stood, phone in hand, calling the police.

"I'll take that," he said, sliding the phone out of her hand.

Chapter Five

Luckily, there was the pinky promise.

"What's a pinky promise?" the boy asked.

"An inviolable oath."

"What inviolable oath?"

"You can't come over."

"I can't?"

"No."

"Never?"

"Never."

So they arranged to meet at his house, a three-bedroom place at the opposite end of town. He opened the door and Anna stepped into chaos so dark and primitive she started taking pictures.

"Why are you taking pictures?" asked the roommate, a tall, willowy specimen with erratic facial hair and no pigmentation. Anna aimed her phone at a pile of dishes by the sink. The boy came out of the shower.

"She's taking pictures," the roommate said. Anna captured a stratum of toothpaste around the bathroom sink.

"Jack, she's taking pictures."

"Why are you taking pictures?"

Balanced on one arm of the couch, Anna shot the mother of all spiderwebs.

"Dude, I'm not sure I want her around, taking pictures like this."

"Put that thing away," the boy said, so she stepped down and took one last picture of him and his dragon, both still wet from the shower.

They were still in bed when she asked him why he'd dropped out of college. The boy flipped onto his back.

"I'd had enough. Psychology 101? Please. We're running out of potable water."

"So you aim to dig wells?"

"I don't aim to dig wells, no. I aim to ride my bike, I aim to ski, I aim to surf, I aim to paraglide. I aim to live. That's what I aim to do: *live*."

"What happens when we run out of water?"

"I trade my bike for a shovel and the rest for a gun."

For a second Anna was tempted to instruct the young man in the way things used to be, to lay out before his astonished eyes the entirely logical expectation that—barring exceptional circumstances typically to do with previously accumulated wealth—the new generations would enter the workforce as soon as humanly possible and contribute, through the acquisition of financial security, to the progress of the human race. It took only the briefest look in the boy's direction to determine the crushing futility of *any* instruction, no matter the type.

"I don't know," she said. "A degree is a degree."

"A degree is not what I was put on this planet for."

"I see. What were you put on this planet for?"

"Right now," he said, rolling on top of her, "for you." And while the attention pleased her, Anna couldn't help but privately lament the transformation of an entire generation of would-be men into drifters and vagabonds.

She'd had the conversation with Richard Strand, of all people. He'd married at age twenty-five. By age twenty-seven, he'd held his first son in his arms. Richard Strand came from money but, still, upon marriage he'd secured a job at a bank and brought in his first paycheck. Later he'd opened a restaurant, worked eighteen-hour days, cajoled waitstaff and dishwashers, upgraded to a full liquor license, brought in chefs, changed menus, made big bucks.

"It was never a thought," he'd said to her, "never a thought that you wouldn't get a job and work your ass off. You had to work your ass off. You had to make money. You had a wife who wasn't making any money. You had a kid who was a couple decades away from making any money. You had to make money. Then women started making money and look what happened."

"Drifters," said Anna.

"Vagabonds," said Richard Strand.

*   *   *

69

Later that day, Anna and Ree examined the contents of six photographs on Anna's phone. Ree shook her head. "I'd get a tetanus shot before going back in, man."

"It's like the apocalypse, the second coming. What kind of person manifests this kind of mayhem?"

"A kid who just dropped out of college?"

"I don't know. I nearly dropped out of college. No place I ever lived in looked remotely like this."

"He's a guy. A guy living with two other guys. What are they like, by the way?"

"Major overachievers. Future pillars of the community. One picks up trash for a living, the other one grooms dogs."

"What about him?"

"He waits tables." They sat in silence as a shot of primordial slime on the living room carpet faded slowly to black.

"Why did he drop out?"

"We're running out of potable water."

Ree gave her a long, uncritical look. "I get it," she said, "I get it. What's he going to do with a degree in accounting when we end up with no water?"

"What's he going to do with his bike?"

"Same thing as a degree in accounting," said Ree, "but after a shit ton of fun."

At home, Esperanza and Eva had the cleaning channel on. "Mamma, you need to get Espi Mop & Glo."

Suddenly attuned to the elapsing nature of things, to the

brittle ecology of all sanctuaries, Anna was quick to acquiesce. She needed these two sitting on the couch, she needed the improbable blues and oranges of the cleaning channel, she needed the dog staring miserably from under his brown cap with holes for his ears, she needed them inside with her and the rest of it outside, cast out, banished like the dark to the outer edges of her property, where the coyotes skulked and screamed and a wolf had once made a ghostly appearance in the middle of a storm, sitting immobile for hours under a thickening mantle of snow.

"I don't like tomatoes," Eva said at dinner, and Anna nearly gave her little girl a standing ovation, so in keeping with tradition was the objection.

"Eat your dinner," Esperanza said, spearing a fingerling potato and examining it from every angle and in this way confirming the solidity of their arrangement, the fixity of time and space within the narrow confines of their dining room.

"What did you do today?" Eva asked in her little voice. Esperanza, whom Anna had burdened with a full confession, shot Anna a quick look but said nothing.

Fork in midair, Anna stared. "What did I do?"

Eva raised her eyes. "Yes. What did you do?"

"Don't ask your mother what she did," said Esperanza. "It's none of your business what your mother did."

Eva looked from one to the other. "Don't ask her? She's my *mother*."

"That don't mean nothing," Esperanza said, and in the

71

silence that fell, for the first time since the big move out West, past and future failed to meet in the present. Separated by a crack lengthening with a low lament down the dinner table, the past stood as a monument to clarity and congruity while the future began to twist and turn darkly upon itself like some shapeless thing come to exact some price. What could Anna say? I *feasted* on a human body? I sank my hands wrist-deep into a human heart and suffered the same encroachment in return? I traced the outlines of a boy's dragon with my tongue? I died a thousand deaths so I could come back to life?

"Mom."

"What?"

"I want to know what you did today."

Anna looked at Esperanza, whose inspection of the potato was far from over, cleared her lungs, speared her own potato, and said, "I went to the movies."

"The movies? What did you see?"

"What did I see?"

Eva nodded, her eyes bright.

"I saw *Raiders of the Lost Ark.*"

"Mom."

"What?"

"That movie is, like, a hundred years old."

"It was a retrospective."

"What's a retrospective?"

"When they show old things. They're showing all the Indiana Jones movies."

Eva's eyes lit up. "Can I go? I want to go."

"It was the last one."

"But that's the first one."

"They went backward."

"Mom."

"What?"

"You're lying."

"Me?"

"Yes."

"Why would I lie?"

"I don't know."

Esperanza put her fork down. "Who's coming to Sonic?"

"Me!" yelled Eva.

Alone at the dinner table, Anna cradled her forehead with one hand and sat in the pulsating silence of her home, in the whiteness of her empty shell, for a long time before getting up and slowly going to the phone.

"I've just lied to Eva for the first time, Mia, a stupid little lie, but a dirty lie nonetheless. After everything the girl's been through, you'd imagine I'd spare her the indignity, but there you have it. I'm calling because I want your voice mail to record for posterity that I am not going near that boy again. I'm not going to his place, and I'm not having him over. In fact, I'm not having anybody over. Not even you, Mia. If you were to do a Lazarus and come back from the dead or wherever you are, we'd still have to meet for coffee in town."

And she made good. For days all entreaties went unanswered, access was denied to young and old alike. She switched to herbal tea instead of coffee in the morning, she

73

went to the farmers' market and purchased a forest of greens that she parceled out to her neighbors the next day. She clipped her toenails and sloughed her feet to avoid further censure from her yoga teacher, who had reluctantly relayed a message from a woman so revolted by Anna's hooves that she'd quit her practice and left the studio in a rage.

Then Mia called.

"Back from the dead," said Anna.

"What dead? I was in Brazil."

"You went to Brazil?"

"You forgot I was going to Brazil?"

"I did. How was Brazil?"

"Full of lovely Brazilians and their lovely children. How's my angel?"

"Good. She's running for president of the dog."

"Tell her she has my vote."

"I cut my toenails. I sloughed my feet."

"That should improve your standing for a while."

Anna smiled. They'd started down the ashtanga yoga path together, Mia progressing smoothly to the end of the first series, Anna cursing her way from injury to injury until the final surrender and the humble new beginning. Mia had moved into the second series by then. She had memorized the name of every posture in Sanskrit and added to her repertoire a lengthy final prayer, also in Sanskrit, whose hypnotic, painfully redemptive closure consisted of the word *shanti*—the peace that surpasseth understanding—chanted three times.

At first Anna had failed to understand. She had practiced

in New York, Boston, Los Angeles, Chicago, Seattle, Denver, Santa Fe, and Taos. The ashtanga studios of America were packed with all-star athletes outdoing each other in the name of yoga. Only in her tiny studio on Morada Lane—a single room where orchids bloomed all year round and silence condensed like matter around human breath—had Anna truly rested in the heart of the practice. To the people who came from out of town to dazzle, to impress, her teacher—a lunar creature with eyes like pools of amber—would say, "Lie down. Find your breath. You'll be doing better yoga that way."

Mia was a curious blend when she'd shown up. She was clearly unconcerned by the performance of others and yet so obsessed with her own that Anna had looked upon her with some suspicion. It hadn't taken long to figure out that every extra effort she put into the practice was in the service of a religious ritual, an exercise of absolute devotion. She had a good way of putting it, a solid way of putting it. "Without this practice," she'd say, "I'd be smashing bottles into the wall."

Mia had a ridiculously successful marriage, but she also had a thing about Persephone, who was dragged down into the underworld by Hades and there enslaved and raped. Nothing in her childhood suggested exposure to trauma on that level, but Mia was raised on a ranch, in the spare world of horses and cattle, fences and gates, dry manure, constantly rising dust. She was raised in a world where little life moved and where her drawings—pencil first, charcoal later—drew pitying smiles from the women, savage laughter from the men. "You gonna eat that, honey? You gonna *day-gest* that, baby girl? Get the calories you need to pull that gate shut?" And because she'd loved that world, she'd lingered in it far too long—coming out of it a fury.

"Look at that idiot, that knucklehead."

"Where?"

"Over by the cash register."

It was early in the morning, not long after they'd first met. The coffee shop was full. Anna squinted and eventually brought into focus a relatively benign-looking man in a pert cowboy hat.

"What did he do?"

"His wife just asked him for twenty bucks and he said no."

Anna took a second look. The man was putting his money clip away. There didn't seem to be much in it.

"Here, darlin'," he said, handing his wife a tall Americano.

Mia shook her head. "Fucking men," she said.

A couple of weeks later, in the same coffee shop, after enduring a leisurely stare from a total stranger for what had clearly been a minute too long, Mia took the man's cup of coffee and poured it in the trash. The man jumped out of his seat.

"You got a problem with that?" asked Mia.

"Yeah, I got a problem with that, that's my fucking coffee, you crazy bitch."

"Didn't your momma teach you not to stare? No? She didn't? Well, *somebody's got to teach you not to stare.*"

And maybe six months after that, down in Santa Fe, at a stage when Anna had begun to physically maneuver Mia away from all potential offenders, including bent-over old men with walking canes, three lads in suits and ties had watched them come in and strategically positioned themselves next to them at the bar. Anna had purchased a drink and kept her eyes glued to it. Mia had turned to one of the men.

"What are you standing here for?"

"I was thinking we might strike up a conversation."

"Do I look like I'm in a mood to talk?"

"I can't tell, honey. It's kinda dark in here."

"Do I look like you can call me honey?"

The man had cast around for aid. "I guess not," he'd said.

"You can call me 'ma'am.' And you can leave me the fuck alone."

Hence, the yoga practice.

"Where's the boy?" asked Mia.

"In his lair."

"Doing what?"

Anna sighed. "Fumigating, one would hope."

"Have you had sex?"

"We have."

"*And?*"

"And I'm too old for this shit. I should be sloughing my feet, keeping the peace. Did you really tell me you were going to Brazil?"

"You booked Corumbao for me."

"As I was saying, I'm too old."

"Come for dinner. I'm all about *caipirinhas* these days."

In the casual comfort of Mia's dining room, under the casual spell of her mellow marriage to a man *exactly* her age, Anna renewed her vow: no commerce with the boy, no matter the cost.

"Does Richard know?" Mia said, pulling out a cigarillo.

"No."

"Maybe you should tell him."

"Are you kidding? He'll shoot me."

"Not if you shoot him first. You seen his last one?"

"The one with the orange hair?"

"Blue and white."

"You're behind. The blue-and-white one got the boot."

"Why?"

"She put out her cigarette on his leather couch. She was a Gnostic, an early Christian, and a firm believer in putting out her cigarettes on his furniture."

Mia let out a tendril of bluish smoke. "You sure he doesn't know?"

"Nah."

"How can you be sure?"

"He would have called."

Eva was fast asleep later that night, Esperanza in front of the television, when the phone rang.

"Now?" asked Anna.

"Now."

Richard Strand was in the kitchen making chicken *mole,*

filling the house with the deep, sweet scent of melting chocolate.

"Have a seat," he said, and Anna lowered herself onto the same stool of that untroubled night in May, wishing desperately she could turn back the hands of time.

"Can I get you something to drink?"

"A shot of vodka. Actually, two. Two shots of vodka."

Richard Strand went to the freezer, took out a bottle of vodka, and poured out a double for himself, a thimbleful for her. "Cheers," he said, and they actually clinked glasses before he pierced her with a stare so cold and resolute that she considered a clean leap out the kitchen window.

"Jack is my *son*," Richard Strand said. "Did you know Jack is my son?"

"Of course I know Jack is your son."

"So what do you think you're doing with my son?"

Anna lowered her eyes.

"Look at me. My son is twenty years old. How old are you?"

"Richard . . ."

"Answer the question. How old are you?"

"Old," she said sharply, holding his stare. "And you? How old are you? I mean specifically in relation to the half-naked high schoolers I keep seeing around here."

Richard picked up a wooden spoon, turned to the melting chocolate. "I'm making chicken *mole*. My son loves chicken *mole*," and in his voice, impossible to miss, were both the yearning and the distance, the unmistakable signs of an impossible pursuit. She drained the vodka as Richard went on stirring, releasing traces of cinnamon and cumin along with his own deep need. For what? thought Anna. For the reconstituted dream? For the exalted return to the place that never was? The boy's only reference to his father had been short and not particularly sweet, some barbed remark about the number of barely legal girls Richard Strand had installed in his home and in his children's lives.

"He came to my house once," she said softly. "I went to his house once. I haven't seen him since."

Richard Strand turned and glared.

"I know what went on," he said. "You don't have to tell me what went on. I have a son who's a wreck and a friend who doesn't give a damn."

Anna pulled back, surprised. "A wreck? How could he be a wreck?"

"He's *a kid,* Anna, *a kid.*"

"Fuck."

"Yeah," Richard Strand said between tight teeth. "Literally and figuratively."

"All right, let's strive for a degree of civility."

"Civility? You call what you did to my son *civil?*"

"I didn't do anything to your son."

"You fucked him. You fucked him and you dumped him and you did it knowing that he was *my son.* How about I send somebody along to fuck your daughter up? How does that grab you?"

Anna was off her stool before she knew it.

"Watch what comes out of your mouth."

"You watch your hormones."

The two stood facing one another until Richard laid a heavy hand on her shoulder and said, "Just talk to him, explain to him. Don't just drop him like some piece of trash. He's *my son*."

"Richard, there's nothing to talk about. He's twenty, I'm forty-two. End of story."

"End of story, my ass. You started it. You wrote the first chapter, you wrote the second chapter. Now write an ending that is respectful of who my son is and how far he's come."

"How far he's come? Richard, I don't know your son from a hole in the ground. I have no idea how far he's come."

"Well, *find out,* why don't you."

"I can't," Anna said, fighting a wave of panic. "I can't be around him, I'm sorry, but it's not something I can do. Please don't make me explain. It should be obvious enough."

Richard Strand went back to stirring. For a while no one spoke. Then Richard turned to face her. "He needs to hear that. You're not getting involved with my son again, but he needs to hear that."

"Richard . . ."

"Make sure he hears that."

She called the boy, and they agreed to meet at the southern-most coffee shop in town, past the church of Saint Francis of Assisi, where immediately after their move Anna and Eva had spent every Sunday morning between nine and ten—Eva doodling in her red notebook, bored by the priest, Anna staring up at the bruised, bleeding god wondering how someone as badly fucked up as that could lend assistance just then.

"God will help us," she kept telling Eva, who'd pierce her with her indigo eyes and say things like, "But if God is in the trees, how can he help us?"

"Who told you God is in the trees?"

"My teachers at school. They say God is in the air and in the trees. They say he's inside me and inside you."

"Inside you, maybe."

"You too, Mom."

"I don't know about that."

"Mom."

"Okay, okay."

"Say it."

"What?"

"Inside me and inside you."

"Inside me and inside you."

"And the trees."

"Screw the trees. There can't possibly be enough to go around."

In church, those empty mornings, Anna had the time to revisit the day her life had fallen apart. Like walking through an empty house in the dead time before dawn, she moved from moment to moment as if from room to room—past smoky mirrors, daybeds shrouded in white linen—toward a door and a bed by an open window on which two bodies lay asleep. Time and time again in her memory she stopped at the door, knowing what she would find but not knowing if her heart could take it. Time and time again she went ahead so those pale limbs entwined in sleep could catch fire in her imagination and remind her why she had put a continent plus an ocean between Eva's father and herself—why there was no going back.

Years slipped past without a single reference to their desperate departure until one afternoon, on the way to soccer practice, Eva said, "I want my daddy to take me to soccer."

Oblivious to the tempest raging in her little girl's heart, Anna had shrugged.

"The likelihood is small."

"Why?"

"Your father lives on a different continent."

"He lives on a different continent because you left him! You left him and now I don't have a dad!"

"Your father cheated on me, Eva."

"No he didn't!"

"Yes, he did. He cheated on me."

"My daddy doesn't cheat!"

"No? Go ahead and ask him. Ask him why I left."

"Liar! You're a liar!" her little girl screamed, and out of nowhere, impetuous and wild and absolute in its desolation, came a flood of tears—sobbing so deep and uncontrolled Anna felt like ripping her own teeth out.

It had never come up again, not once. Like a confession before a priest, the exchange had grown faint and seemed to have left no trace in time.

Now, the church came into view and impulsively Anna stopped, got out, and galloped toward the door, pulling on the handle with a smile, only to find it locked. She stepped back in disbelief. A locked church was like a turned grave; it spoke of some violation, some desecration, not just the breach of an agreement but a betrayal, an omission bordering on outrage. Resisting the urge to beat on the door with both fists, Anna slid to the ground and sat there, knees against chest, pursuing distant flocks of birds with tired eyes until the moment came, and she got up.

There was no one in the café, only the boy. He was slumped on a chair like a boxer between rounds, looking at her out of eyes that were impossible to meet. She had rehearsed her speech. It was going to be short and businesslike, drained of emotion, free of apology. But when she opened her mouth not a sound came out. He shifted in his seat and she caught a glimpse of the dragon against the whiteness of his flesh. She'd forgotten how creamy his skin was, how smooth against her own. She had forgotten how beautiful he was, how strong, how tall, and before she could help herself she had a hand on his knee, her forehead on his shoulder. He was rigid at first, cold and unyielding at first, but gradually he turned on his chair so she could slide one leg over his knees and straddle him and their mouths could meet—and they could kiss.

Chapter Six

It was mid-June when Eva left. Water ran low and slow in the *acequias*, the air was thick with sun dust and juniper pollen. Aspen leaves had thickened and darkened and now danced delirious in the wind.

Anna, Eva, and Esperanza set out in the middle of the night across a searing emptiness so Eva could fly out of Phoenix and get to the other side of the continent on a nonstop flight and, from there, fly on to London. The sun found Anna at the wheel, Esperanza snoring in the passenger seat, Eva prim and erect in the backseat, a map over her little legs, eyes fixed maniacally on the road ahead.

"I don't understand. What have I done? What have I ever done to leave you with such little confidence in my driving skills?"

"Mom, look at the road."

"I'm looking at the road."

"No, you're looking at me, look at the road."

They stopped three times total—once because Esperanza had tears in her eyes from the pressure on her bladder but, faced with the indignity of squatting by the car in partial view of traffic, settled mutely in her seat again, closing her eyes like the martyrs of her religion—and they got to the airport five hours before departure.

"Go have fun," Anna said, tossing Esperanza the car keys.

"Are you crazy?" yelled Eva. "She'll go gamble!"

The two women looked at the child.

"Hija," Esperanza cut in haughtily, "I have no money to gamble *with.*"

The two hugged with surprising formality, and it was only thanks to an unplanned backward glance that Anna caught a furtive tear sliding down Esperanza's cheek. "Wave to Espi," Anna said. Eva waved.

"Wave a little harder."

"Mom."

"You're hurting her feelings. Wave."

"I'm waving."

"Jesus. Will you remember *my* name when you get back?"

Only at the gate did Eva's senior citizen façade come crumbling down. She clung polyp-like to her mother's arm.

"Please, Mamma," she pleaded through a mask of tears, "I don't want to be with Daddy, I want to be with you." It took the personal intervention of the captain to get her on the walkway.

"Don't forget to feed Paco," were her parting words, shouted with a broken voice. "And fix the brakes, okay, Mamma? Promise me you'll fix the brakes."

Esperanza had to be paged by airport security and was belligerently drunk by the time they hooked up at baggage carousel number four. "Stole my money," she said, spitting on the floor. "Fucking Indians stole my fucking money."

Anna drove in silence through a fantasy of gradually graying rock until the New Mexico border, when Esperanza awoke from a dead sleep and said, "We should have a border, no? How come we don't have no border?"

"It's the same country, Esperanza."

"No it's not. I know history, that country is Indian country." Anna shrugged.

"I know history," Esperanza said. "That thing back there is Indian country."

Anna took the car to the shop the next day and was treated to a stinging display of hostility. "You're lucky to be alive," the mechanic said, tossing her the keys.

Her little girl called from London. "You fixed the brakes?"

"Yes, my love."

"Were they bad?"

"Yes, my love."

"I *told* you."

"I know, my love."

The boy kept calling and Anna kept standing there watching the phone ring, incapable of lifting the receiver.

She could conjure only fragments of what his presence in a house without Eva would bring: his smell on her sheets, his music on her stereo, the collapse of time, the erasure of time, the thinning out of sounds, the muting of voices, the heartbreak of flesh against flesh—and she was ready for none of it.

"I nearly killed my little girl driving up to Phoenix, my brakes were so bad," she informed Mia's machine. "Don't go to Phoenix, by the way, no point in ever setting foot in Phoenix. The guy at the car shop was appalled. He asked me if I had children. I said no. He said, 'Haven't I seen you with a little blondie?' I said, 'Me? A little blondie? Look at me, I've got Bedouin blood.' He gave me a dirty look. The guy's got children. His brakes don't need fixing."

Mia called back within half an hour. "I know the guy. He beats his wife."

"He beats his wife?"

"Kicks the shit out of her."

"How do you know?"

"Have you *seen* her?"

"No."

"That's all you have to do. Take a look at her."

"That's terrible. I was just saying, though, I should have gotten those brakes fixed sooner."

"Not by that motherfucker."

Summer progressed, Eva was gone, judgment suspended, so it wasn't long before the phone rang again, and Anna took the call.

"What are you doing?" Eva asked her mother the next time they spoke.

"Nothing," Anna said, watching the boy come out of the bathroom with a towel around his waist.

"Nothing? You must be doing *something*."

"I swear to God, I'm doing nothing." The boy approached, his intentions clear, and she waved him furiously away but he sank slowly to his knees and ran his hands up her calves.

"Mom," she heard Eva say as if through a fog, "you never just do *nothing*."

"I do too."

And her little *witch,* her little magician, her miniature Merlin, from across a continent and the incalculable density of an ocean said, "Is somebody there?"

Anna shot to her feet. "Is somebody here? Why would someone be here?"

"Mom."

"What?"

"You're sounding all strange."

"I'm sounding strange? What about you? Are you picking up a British accent?"

"Mom, I'm in Britain."

"I know you're in Britain, but that doesn't mean you have to pick up a British accent. I'm leaving you at baggage claim if you come back with a British accent. You can hitchhike home."

"Daddy says I sound like a Yank."

"Don't listen to a word your father says. You know what he's like."

"I know," Eva sighed. "Daddy's irresponsible."

"Crazy irresponsible. Off the charts irresponsible."

"It's what he says about you."

"Like I said, don't listen to a word your father says."

She emerged from sleep the next morning in a different skin, both lighter from the touch of the boy's hands and heavier with the awareness of some ineluctable slide. She turned to face him and recoiled. She'd never seen him asleep before and she was out of bed before she knew it. This was not the integrated man-boy she had fallen for, not the thing standing loosely in his body; this was a child pushing up from childhood, a changeling called upon to impress a tender geography of bone and memory into the cramped, unyielding mold of manhood.

She was in the kitchen staring at nothing when he came in.

"What's wrong?" he asked.

"You're a child," she said.

He said nothing. He took her by the hand and pulled her back to bed, covering her body with his, pinning her head between his elbows, letting his mouth fall open slowly against hers. In the silence of the ripening day, she traced every ridge, every curve of the boy's body, committing to memory not the body but the soul before its sure alteration.

"The die is cast," she said.

"The what is what?"

"One die. Two dice."

"One die, two dice. I see. What about the die?"

"It's cast. *Alea jacta est.* I had to study Latin, long story. Do you know who Caesar was?"

"Yeah, the Roman guy."

"The Roman guy. Do you know what he did?"

"He got stabbed."

"That too, that too. But before that, he took his army across this river called the Rubicon and marched on Rome. His chances of success were ridiculously low but, like he said before crossing the Rubicon, the die was cast."

The boy ran a slow hand through her hair. "Good attitude," he said.

"Can you blame me?"

"I can and I do."

Anna let her gaze drift to the window. "Your father is going to flay and quarter me."

"My father," said the boy, "needs to learn how to mind his own business."

"He's your father."

Leaning back against the pillows, folding his face into a caricature of distress, the boy raised his voice to a falsetto. "Are you okay, buddy? You okay? Should we cut down that tree you keep falling out of? Eat frozen food so you don't burn your hand? Get rid of that second story so you don't keep going down the stairs on your fucking head while I'm doing little Bunny over here doggy style in the next room?"

Anna stared, her breath caught in her throat. "Your father *raised* you."

"My father did no such thing. Age four, I packed my own lunch."

Anna cleared her throat. "Your father was younger then."

"Age *four*. If I didn't pack my lunch, no one would pack my lunch."

"We make mistakes," Anna said.

"I don't give a fuck. Mistakes, no mistakes, that's in the past. But this, this is *my* business, okay? My business. Not his."

"He's worried about you. Your father is worried about you."

He sank his fingers into her arms. "Don't you get it? I'm in this. I'm in this for real. I'm *never* letting go."

"Christ," Ree said. "Is that what you *wanted?*"

They were at the sushi place having lunch. Anna let out a sigh.

"I don't know. I don't know what I wanted."

Ree poked her seaweed suspiciously with a chopstick. "Well," she said, "you've got it."

"Got what?"

"I don't know."

"Will you stop *poking* the fucking thing and eat it?"

Ree lifted a single strand of pickled seaweed to her nose and sniffed it. "I don't know about this."

"Why did you order it?"

"I don't know."

"Because you're stoned. You thought you were ordering something else."

Ree raised her green untroubled eyes to meet Anna's. "You're absolutely right. And you know what? I'm not eating this shit. So. You've got it. What are you going to do with it?"

"I don't know."

"No?"

"No." The two sat staring out at the sacred mountain, the site of a million pilgrimages under the great New Mexican sky.

"I've got premonitions," Anna said. "Intimations of disaster."

"Oh shit," said Ree.

"Oh shit is right."

"It's like something out of Aristotle."

"Sophocles."

"Aristotle."

"Aristotle's the philosopher."

Ree lifted a chopstick against the light, measuring out a corner of heaven with it. "Whatever," she said.

Summer advanced with the subtle power of amnesia, and soon no covenant was safe. Every day Esperanza complained about some item she hadn't seen before. A baseball cap. A new iPod. Handfuls of change. Spectacularly, one day, a bong.

"You should see it," Anna told Dr. Roemer. "The thing's on wheels."

"Are you happy?"

"I can't tell."

The doctor picked something off his shirt. "I'm not surprised."

"No?"

He shook his head. "No."

"Why not?"

"No one can make you happy."

Truth reveals itself through absence, absence through truth. Sitting in the doctor's office, pierced by a stare so ancient there was no placing it in time, Anna felt herself crash into a zero moment of total certainty. It lasted only a second but the outlines remained, lingering in the form of a slow suspicion, a pale doubt.

"What are you talking about?" she said. "You're married. You've been married twenty years."

"Yes, but the minute I start depending on my wife for my happiness, I'm screwed. The minute I wake up and think, I hope my wife is in a good mood otherwise I'm screwed, I'm screwed. No one can make you happy. Only the thinking in your head can make you happy."

Anna checked her nails; they were disgusting. She always checked her nails, and they were always disgusting.

"Why do you feel the need to get so dogmatic with me all the time?"

"Dogmatic?"

"Dogmatic, imperial. What's the problem here? You're married, I've got a boy staying at my house, no one's upset, it's all good, but you're lecturing me. Why are you lecturing me?"

"Because you keep coming in here all fucked up."

"You'd be out of a job if I didn't keep coming in here all fucked up. You should thank me, you should make your gratitude felt."

"Tell me what happens when Eva comes back."

"When Eva comes back?"

The doctor gave her his mandarin look.

"He leaves."

"Just like that?"

Anna looked away.

"He picks up all his stuff and leaves?"

"Something like that."

"Come on. Can we be serious for once?"

Anna shot to her feet. "What do you want from me? Tell me what you want from me."

Seconds ticked past, silence thickening around them like a shroud.

"Why do you pay me?" said the doctor.

"Who knows? Who knows why I pay you."

"You're free to leave, Anna. Door's right there."

"Look," she said, sitting back down. "All I want is a break. I have led the life of an indentured servant. I have been reduced in every possible, conceivable way to the role of a *caregiver*. What about me? Who takes care of me? I'm tired, Doctor Roemer. I have been constrained beyond all reasonable parameters, I have been enslaved, shackled like some goddamned convict and I'm tired. I *need* this. I need it more than words could possibly begin to express."

"Well," the doctor said, leaning back in his chair, touching his fingertips together, "you've got it."

*   *   *

Strangely, it rained, and to placate Esperanza, who hated the rain and the boy with total impartiality, Anna left the boy at home and drove them to Las Vegas, where she sat for three days with a magazine she never opened by a pool without a deep end. Esperanza raged like a brushfire past her on a couple occasions, and when they finally hooked up in the lobby for the trip back home, she had the breath of a dragon, the eyes of an assassin.

"What did you steal?" said Anna as soon as they were in the car. "You must have stolen something to keep going like that."

Wasted beyond speech, Esperanza produced a sound between a grunt and a chuckle and passed out cold. When she came to, hours later, Anna had catalogued her findings over three days of complete inertia.

"How can he *not know* what went on in World War Two. Fifty million people died in World War Two. Fifty million. That's a shitload of people, Esperanza, a shitload, but we live in an age where the volume of information available is so massive, the stream so deafening, that kids today are separated, mentally and emotionally separated, from what went on last month, forget fifty, sixty years ago. Is it a good separation? I don't think so. The Second World War defines who I am in a very concrete way: the mass graves, the death marches, the gas chambers, the aerial bombings, the gutting of an entire continent. How can a college kid not know about this shit? What is it that these kids know about? They know how to download a video from YouTube while updating their status on Facebook. They know how to send one hundred text messages a day and disfigure the English language in the process. The rest they know nothing about. Nothing. Zero. It's as if it never happened."

Esperanza sat there looking like she'd been hit with a stun gun.

"Eee," she said. "Why do you get all upset? Don't get so upset." But the second they got home she gave the boy a tight black smile and said, "Find out what happened in World War Two, *hijo*."

"Why do I need to find out what happened in World War Two?"

"Don't know," Anna said, kissing him softly on the neck. "Seems like a biggie to me."

The Fourth of July came and, with it, an astonishing parade of people reclined, barely awake by the look of it, on their motorcycles. Esperanza added a fourth layer of hair gel and disappeared. In the days that followed, Anna lost track of time, lost track of herself, allowing the boy to wash her hair in the shower, shedding her clothes in favor of his, wearing his jeans, his shirts. He stood in the kitchen while she washed his dishes.

"I want my shirt back," he said. Their eyes met.

"Now?"

"Now."

She turned, undid the first button.

"Slowly," the boy said. "I want my shirt back slowly."

Chapter Seven

They lay in bed, separated by nothing for hours, and there were times when Anna swore she could feel the boundaries of her skin loosen and dissolve, times when she felt his secrets slip under her tongue and rest there. How he slept: on his back, his arms thrown over his head. What moved him: the flight paths of birds—there was one directly over her house, she'd never noticed—the exact spot where the Rio Hondo crashed into the Rio Grande and there gave up its soul with a visible shudder. The way he used his fork and knife, with surgical, suffocating precision, contrasted to the way he held his beer, with a slack wrist. The nearly mechanical steadiness of his young breath. His long, long silences—empty spaces strikingly void of expectation, placid parentheses in which his need for words simply disappeared.

"Tell me what you're thinking," she would ask him.

"Later."

"Tell me something."

"Later."

In the silence of the house, his mysteries became her own. The childhood dreams he had of becoming an astronaut until he heard David Bowie describe Major Tom's cold drift into space. The realization, early in high school, that a particle behaved differently if observed or left alone.

"Where'd you read that?" Anna asked.

"In every physics book printed since Heisenberg."

"Who's Heisenberg?"

"The guy who ran the experiment."

"What experiment?"

"An electron coming through an opening either as a particle or as a wave depending if somebody is watching."

"You're making this up."

"Why would I make something like this up?"

"Because you're a kid. Kids make stuff up."

"Yeah?" he said, sliding one finger under her bra strap. "What kind of stuff?"

Late in the morning one day, he let his forearm fall heavily over his eyes and said, "I used to think I had the best father in the world. The tall, dashing guy who showed up in a convertible, music blaring, and whisked you away from baseball practice with all your friends watching, wishing they, too, had a dad like that."

"I don't want to hear it," she said, and she really didn't want to hear it, but the boy had perfected the art of ignoring her at all the right junctures so he just went on.

"Then I got to college and I fell in this hole and, when I came out, there was this rage, this fucking *rage*. And it had to do with my father. My mother was, like, never there, but at least she was *never there,* you know? You could pat her on the head and up her dose of lithium and she'd only smile at you. My father came in and out of my life like a fucking tornado and it was always about *him*. 'Hey, bud, how about we go hit some balls and get a cocktail?' 'Hey, bud, I got tickets to *Friday the 13th*. Big, bad, scary movie but don't worry, I'll sneak you in.' Friday the fucking thirteenth? I couldn't sleep for years. Years."

"We make mistakes," she said quietly.

"Yeah. *Big* mistakes."

"No one's perfect, Jack."

"There are *degrees* of imperfection."

"Nothing could be truer. Absolutely nothing. Can we drop it now?"

"Yeah," the boy said, getting out of bed. "We can drop it."

He was peering into the fridge—a morning ritual of alarming length, as if the food were hard to locate, or possibly situated somewhere else—when she came in.

"Why don't you take him out?" she said.

He turned his head slowly. "Take who out?"

"Your father. Drive a stake into his heart. Get it over with."

The boy straightened, shut the refrigerator door with a sigh.

"Guess who's getting all crazy again."

"The man paid your bills. He put a roof over your head. He

put food on the table. He toiled endlessly so *you* could drop out of college. And he's the guy who ruined your life?"

"Anna."

"What?"

"Come here."

The bikers left town, and Esperanza reemerged with a conscience so dirty she picked up a rag and started scrubbing the minute she walked through the door.

"I need more rags," she said. "And bleach. I need more bleach."

At the store, Ree's cart was predictably empty. "I pull in here and I get my cart and I start looking around and suddenly I've got no idea why I'm here."

"Were you purchasing sustenance for your children?" asked Anna.

"That's what I'm assuming, I just don't know what. And you know what I'm thinking? I'm thinking it's because I'm tired of cooking. I used to run a manufacturing plant in China and all I do is cook. What about you? Do you cook all the time?"

"Some of the time."

"Haven't we had this conversation before?"

"We have."

"Remind me again. Who cooks when you don't?"

"Eva."

"Eva? She's *eight*."

"She *wanted* to do it. She was desperate to do it. Age six she started harassing me. First it was coffee. Then it was scrambled eggs. Then it was pancakes. Now she makes bread."

"You're shitting me."

"I am not shitting you."

"Grace couldn't boil an egg if I boiled it *for* her."

Anna gave her a sympathetic nod then, suddenly overcome by the molecular imperative to hear her daughter's voice, she pulled out her cell phone and ran out of the store.

She had to go through the girl's father, of course. He answered the phone with typical boorishness. "Oh hello, Anna. Why, yes, Eva is standing right here."

"Let me speak to her."

"I'm very well, thank you for asking. And you? Are you in jail? In an asylum? Or should we be so bold as to set our sights on a halfway house?"

"Yeah, yeah, yeah. Let me speak to my daughter."

"Rumor has it you were caught snogging a twenty-year-old. I told Eva she'd be wise to keep an eye on her little playmates when she gets back."

"God, how funny. How about you? Still with the Nobel laureate?"

"Nothing wrong with a trophy wife, nothing wrong. At least she's legal."

"Great talking to you. Put Eva on the phone."

"A pleasure as always. Eva, your barking mother wants to talk to you."

Anna's heart warmed at Eva's high-pitched protest. "My mother is not barking! Mamma! Hey, my Mamma!"

"What are you doing with that criminal, that lunatic, that threat to society?"

"Daddy's fine. He's just had a bit to drink."

"Is he driving?"

"Mom!"

"Answer the question. Is he driving?"

"No, he's not driving!"

"No? Who's driving, then?"

"The driver."

"Oh," said Anna, instantly reduced to the core of her penniless state.

"What are you doing?"

"Well," chirped Eva, clearly in great spirits, "we've just had dinner and we're meeting David for after-dinner drinks."

"David's another one."

"Mom."

"What?"

"I love David."

"What's there to love? The man's got too much money."

"Mom!"

"Eva, darling, come home. I can't stand it without you."

"Oh Mom."

"No 'oh Mom.' I'm *nothing* without you, my love, nothing."

Eva giggled, and in the parking lot of the grocery store, alone in the sun's lengthening rays, hours away from slumber, hours away from peace, Anna felt something tear badly in the middle of her.

Anna did not cry. As a rule, as a practice, as an expression of who she was. Tears belonged to the unsettled world of children, to the hazy hemisphere of human madness. Nothing embarrassed her more than an adult crying. It strained every fiber in her body, hardened every cell, drained her of all emotion. Yet there she was, weeping as if at an Irish wake.

"Call you right back," she said but there was no fooling her little Merlin.

"She's crying! Daddy! Mamma's crying!"

"Is she really? How devastating."

"Mamma?"

"I'm fine, my love, I'm fine. I miss you."

"You're fine?"

"I promise."

"How's Espi?"

Esperanza was far from well, having read into the boy's encroachment signs of impending ruin for reasons she darkly described as her own.

"She's a little cranky."

"Why?"

"I don't know. I guess she's broke."

"She's always broke. Did you feed Paco?"

"No."

"Daddy, Mom forgets to feed the dog all the time."

"The dog? Ask her if she's feeding *herself*."

"Daddy wants to know if you're feeding yourself."

She'd had her key in the car door by then. She turned and trotted back to the store. "Of course I'm feeding myself."

*   *   *

Eva's father had come to her place soon after they first met and surveyed her private panorama of two burners, a table, and a chair with clear distaste. He pulled the refrigerator door open and looked down on a bottle of vodka, a bag full of Arabica.

"I don't suppose you can cook," he said.

"Oh yeah, I can cook."

Later that day she put together a meal she dumped steaming hot in the trash.

"Was that rice?" he asked.

"It was."

"How extraordinary. I was wondering what food category that might have once belonged to."

"The rice category."

"How did it acquire that pastel color?"

"Beats me."

"Right," he said, pulling her to him and touching his forehead to hers. "There's a pizza place right down the street." And from that moment on, food had become a world in itself, a place full of silent warnings, issued by none other than herself as she pored over recipe book after recipe book. Never let the oil blacken. Always brown before braising. Steam if you can. Knead at an angle. Stir with rhythm and method. Don't let the blade slip. Don't leave the oven on. And don't forget. Above all, don't walk away and forget.

"Any idea why the oven is on?"

"What oven?"

"The only oven we own, Anna. The one in the kitchen."

"I was going to make something."

"Something to eat, I presume."

"No, something to go bowling with."

"I've never been bowling in my life but I have, on the odd occasion, experienced hunger. Shall we attempt to put something in that oven?"

Or once, on Christmas Day, "Any idea why there's smoke billowing out from under the kitchen door?"

She galloped to the kitchen. "We are so screwed," she said. "So screwed."

"How many people did you invite?"

"Ten."

"Well done. Truly impressive work. Magisterial."

"What about you? Couldn't *you* check the oven? You got some kind of condition preventing you from checking the oven?"

"I don't cook, Anna. The fact can hardly have escaped you."

"Well, learn to fucking cook, why don't you? Here's the recipe book," she said, throwing him the *Larousse Gastronomique*.

It had taken time, time and patience, but in the end she'd developed a sharp sense, a good hand. At least she'd gotten that from trying to please him: the slow, not always smooth, conversion to the earthly merit of food prepared for the pleasure and comfort of others.

*   *   *

Back in the store, Ree had a cooked chicken and a box of crackers in her cart.

"Go to the cheese section. They've got this mango salsa that's out of this world."

"What are you getting, Ree?"

"A cooked chicken. So I don't have to cook it. Were you just crying?"

"I was."

"Is he riding his bike again?"

"He lives in my house, Ree."

"In your house? Did you tell me that?"

"I neglected to mention it."

"What about his father?"

"His father's uninformed."

"I thought he lived next door."

"He does."

"Shit," Ree said. "No wonder you've got premonitions. Does he have a lot of stuff?"

He did. An inexhaustible supply of Boston Red Sox caps, which had a habit of proliferating overnight. Truckloads of loose change. Three cameras, three iPods, two cell phones, two laptops. Shoes. Hiking shoes. Biking shoes. Climbing shoes. Surfing shoes. Jeans. T-shirts. A motorcycle, recently purchased by his father as a reward for dropping out. Two surfboards. A dirt bike. A skateboard crowded with stickers, unsettling testaments to a previous life. A PlayStation, never used. The bong, never washed. Toothbrush. Razor. Shaving cream. A guitar. A few books. Three unopened boxes full of secrets, things he refused to catalogue, even to her. Esperanza attempted to turn them into a *casus belli*, making the hazy case for an inspection on principle alone.

"There could be drugs in there, no? There could be meth from El Rito, no? You know they're making meth in El Rito? We could end up in jail."

"Go for it. Get a box cutter."

"Eee, you're *loca* for this kid, and he's just a kid."

"I'm telling you, go for it."

What was it about the boy that held them both in check? He was tall, tall in the way men are tall over women, comfortably, serenely tall; tall with a broadness and a thickness to him Anna could not begin to relate to, let alone match; tall with a vantage point so different from theirs, endowed with effortless nobility on the strength of verticality alone. But there was also the way he moved around the house, fluid, unhurried, with slow, mindless power. There was the way he sat, legs spread indolently out before him, arm resting on the back of the chair as Anna crossed and uncrossed her legs, her back rigid, her lips pursed.

"It's your house," Esperanza said. "You open them."

"Forget it."

"Eee, you're all crazy, I don't even know how to talk to you anymore."

"Time in the can has never hurt anybody."

"You've never been in the can."

"Oh yes I have."

Esperanza's eyes narrowed. "For what?"

"Drunk driving."

"Eee, that's just one night, no? One night is nothing."

One night, one night only, behind which lay years and years of parched dawns, queasy comings-to in the marshes of uncertainty, countless pushes homeward swerving across yellow lines, five car crashes—all of them in the breaking light of day, when mothers gathered small, warm bodies to their own—a thousand brawls fought on the edge of clinical delusion, once, spectacularly, in Paris, followed by the physical propulsion out of a private club onto unforgiving tarmac. At the hospital, the doctor had shaken his head, *"Elle est folle, celle-ci."*

"Yeah," Anna said, her eyes on the dance of an aspen's leaves. "Just one night."

"One night doesn't count. Santiago Archuleta, my neighbor, no, he got caught for drugs and he's still down in Albuquerque! And his wife can't see him!"

"Why not?"

"I don't know and, with these boxes, you and me, we end up in jail and where's the money for bail? The kid's broke, the kid's got no money, no?"

Money or no money, the kid had taken over in a flash, an instant. She had imagined his possessions to be in proportion to his age, so she had tried to hide her dismay when he'd pulled up in a U-Haul. It was astonishing to her, never mind to Esperanza, how quickly she'd accepted the clutter, how soon she'd held it up daily against the sparseness of her previous life, wondering how she could have ever inhabited such hollow spaces without grief.

Days passed. The boy came and went, shifting the magnetic

field of the house in his direction with every move, every breath, every smile. Determined to reclaim some territory, restore some balance, Anna bought the ingredients to make lasagna. Milk, flour, and butter for the béchamel; onions, carrots, celery, ground beef, veal, and pork for the sauce. She was cubing an onion when the phone rang.

"Hey, Mom."

"Hey, the tiny one! Hey, the little one! Hey, my love! How are you?"

"I'm very well, thank you. How are you?"

"Eva, you can't talk like that."

"Mom."

"Do you have any idea what they're going to do to you in school? The minute you open your mouth?"

"Mom."

"You're not coming home like that. Rent some videos. Watch some American movies. In fact, let me speak to your father."

"Daddy, Mamma wants to speak with you."

"Oh hello, Anna. Are you incarcerated? Do you need money for bail?"

"God, how funny. You're going to send her back sounding like that?"

"Sounding vaguely civil, you mean?"

"You've clearly forgotten, because such minutiae are vastly beneath you, but your daughter is no longer in private school. She's in public school. Public as in public, not private. Yeah? They're going to crucify her."

"Eva, your mother seems to think speaking proper English will get you crucified in school. Small price to pay, I should think, for the privilege of speaking proper English."

"Let me talk to her."

"Always a pleasure, Anna. Always a pleasure."

"Mom?" Eva's voice was uncharacteristically shrill.

"Yes my love."

"Can we please not talk about this?"

"We can, my love. What do you want to talk about?"

"Has Paco been fed?"

"He has."

"What are you doing?"

"I'm cooking."

"Cooking? You never cook!"

"That's because you've usurped my position. Two more weeks, Eva."

"I know. Have you registered me for soccer?"

"I have," Anna said, laying down the knife, wiping her hands, and writing on a board by the fridge, EVA SOCCER!

"Did you get me a new lunch box?"

"A new lunch box? What's wrong with the old one?"

"The handle broke. Remember?"

"Yeah," lied Anna, scrawling LUNCH BOX! "I want you home, Eva."

"I am. I'm coming home," her little girl said.

"We're going to have tons of Mamma-and-me time. I'm going to teach you how to play chess."

"Can we play Wig Out?"

LARA SANTORO

"We're definitively playing Wig Out."

"Daddy says you cheat at cards."

"Your father lies. As a practice, as a principle. Darling, come home."

In her younger days, Anna had often thought that death would come for her quickly, that it would grab her by the neck and shove her under. There would be no time to square her soul to the stars, no time to locate the exit onto the other side. There would be the sudden, irreparable opacity of things, a single unforgiving instant in which every borrowed day would be weighed against not the purity of her soul but against the work of her hands. After Eva's imperial entrance, Anna's beliefs had changed. She would be judged not by the work of her hands but by the quality of sap running up and down her lengthening weed well after she was gone.

"Let me speak to your father again."

"Oh hello, Anna. Still unshackled?"

"Get her *Little House on the Prairie*."

"Which one is that? The one with a whole load of Yanks dressed like Heidi?"

"That's the one."

"Eva, your mother wants you to watch people jumping rope and picking apples. Do you want to watch people jumping rope and picking apples?"

Had the man ever been serious? Had he taken anything remotely seriously in his life? He had come into effortless being with few of the weaknesses, the standard failings of the human heart. Untainted by fear, unconstrained by circumstance, he moved through life as if through a game of something on green grass. While she stood mutely at the foot of her own inadequacies, he soared above the world's open wounds without a single thought of God. There was no stealing his lunch, no getting his goat. She'd seen him cry only once in their history together, at the airport, right before her flight, and even those tears had seemed calculated, manufactured for the occasion.

"Anna, I beg you, don't leave me."

"Fuck you."

"I'll do anything."

"Let go of my arm."

"Anna."

"Eva, it's time to go."

"Daddy."

"Please don't take her away."

"Eva, give me your hand."

"Please."

"Let's go."

"Bye, Daddy."

"I beg you."

"Bye, Daddy."

Anna slid the knife into an onion's flank and dropped it on the board with a sharp intake of breath, blood pooling fast and hard around her fingernail and falling—thick, red, ruby-red—onto the counter.

"Fuck," she said.

"For God's sake, Anna, will you please stop this truck driver business? Eva says you swear all the time."

Anna closed her hand into a fist.

"Will I stop this truck driver business? Will you stop behaving like a fucking two-year-old all the time? Your daughter is coming back to a classroom full of poor, angry kids with crew cuts and a million axes to grind. They will dismember her on arrival."

"Anna, you really must watch the way—"

"I must watch nothing. You get her *Little House on the Prairie.*"

And she hung up.

Silence lapped at her in slow, low waves. She walked into the pantry. Putting out her bloodied hand, she let her fingertips describe the curve of an apple first, an onion next. She lifted an egg. She had forgotten the existence of eggs, the implausible humility of eggs. She had forgotten so much since the boy, let go of so much.

"Hey."

She turned and there was the boy, motorcycle jacket still on despite the heat.

"You're bleeding," he said.

She shrugged.

He didn't provide first aid. He didn't take her by the hand and lead her into the bathroom, search the cabinet, seal the wound. He pressed his thumbs lightly against her lips and brought his mouth to hers.

Chapter Eight

Summer has its own music. It's slow and soft and, more often than not, slightly swollen between notes. Even Esperanza, whose scrubbing had the adrenaline-pumped edge of a full cardiovascular routine, mellowed her game. The boy procured a device through which movies and television shows could be plucked out of the ether and watched online. Anna and Esperanza stood staring at the small black box.

"It's messed up," Anna said.

"It's like witchcraft," Esperanza said. "Where did he get it?"

"I don't know."

"Who paid for it?"

"Who do you *think* paid for it."

"Eee," said Esperanza. "This is starting to be too much."

"You can watch them, too."

"But no, it's not what I'm saying."

"I know what you're saying."

Esperanza shook her head, plunged her hands into her pockets.

"This isn't right. It's just not right. I wash your dishes, I mop your floors, I do your laundry. What does he do?"

"Nothing."

"He eats your food, he lives in your house, he drives your car."

"He does."

"So he owes you money, no?"

"He does."

"Like I owe you money."

"Like you owe me money."

"So he can do the dishes, no? He can do the laundry, no? He can get down on his knees and scrub your toilet, no?"

"Esperanza."

But Esperanza shook her head, dug her hands deeper into her pockets. "This isn't right. It's just not right."

"He's leaving, Espi. He'll be out of here in two weeks."

Esperanza took her hands out of her pockets.

"Don't call me Espi," she said.

Anna took Paco down by the river and sat on a rock watching the golden thing run smiling in and out of the water with a stick in his mouth.

"You've got it easy," she said, and the dog agreed with a sharp bark, a delirious wag of the tail.

"It's messed up."

116

Again, the dog agreed.

"Go fetch!" she said, throwing the dog the stick.

Esperanza was gone when she got home, the boy was stretched on the couch, occupying every angle of the couch, *coating* the piece of furniture like a finish, a veneer, a beer in one hand, the remote in the other.

"Where's Espi?"

He barely looked up.

"I don't know. She left."

"Did she say where she was going?"

The boy hit pause.

"No, she didn't. Why, what happened?"

"You have to start washing some dishes."

The boy put the remote down.

"I have to start washing some dishes?"

"You have to start washing some dishes."

He looked at her with great, almost lofty neutrality, as if the message she had just delivered didn't involve him somehow.

"I have no problem washing dishes."

"No? You have no problem? How come you haven't washed a single one? How has this strange, this honestly puzzling occurrence come to pass? Go ahead. Enlighten me."

"Nobody asked me."

"Nobody asked you. Can't you see? Are you blind? There are dishes in the sink all the fucking time. *All the fucking time.*"

The boy got up.

"All right," he said, "this is where we start calming down. This is where we take a deep breath and start calming down."

And standing there, pushed up against the foulest quarters of her soul, wrapped in rage as in barbed wire, certain of what would come next—the fission, the cleave at nuclear level, the implausible, the unimaginable blast—she looked at him, at his smooth skin, at his clear eyes, at all the things he had yet to live through, all the pain he had yet to feel, and felt herself grow still, and quiet, and afraid.

"I'm sorry," she said.

He took his time, looking at her. Then he put out a hand.

"You maniac," he said.

The phone rang early the next day, and it was Richard Strand.

"I hear my son lives next door."

Anna rolled over and gave the boy the phone. In the kitchen, grinding coffee beans, trying to drown out the sounds from the bedroom, she saw a magpie land fatly on her fence and turn its head sideways with a mechanical jerk. The colors were deafening—cobalt blue, brilliant white, black like a killer whale coming up from the deep—the head tender and fragile beyond what, in Anna's sudden fury, seemed right.

Nothing is right, she thought. Nothing.

The boy came into the kitchen, slapped one hand against the wall.

"Fuck," he said.

"Okay. Let's hear it."

"He started crying."

Anna turned. "Crying?"

"Crying."

"Jesus."

"It's all I need. A grown man crying on the phone."

Anna threw the sponge into the sink. "He's your *father*. Show some fucking respect."

The boy brought his face within an inch of hers. "I show respect to those who *deserve* respect," and barely a minute later she heard the roar of his motorcycle, a nearly audible rising of dust, and then silence.

She took the dog down to the river but kept him close to her this time, hearing, as the wind moved through the canyon, the distant sound of deranged weeping, the legendary keening of *La Llorona*, whose madness it had been to kill her children by drowning them and whose fate, sealed beyond the recall of time, was to walk the water's edge forever calling out their names.

The dog put his head on Anna's lap and closed his eyes. "I know you think she's gone for good," Anna whispered in his ear, "but she's not, she's coming back soon." The dog let out a sigh but seemed much more buoyant on his way home, running in circles around her, barking loudly for his stick, running so fast he went tumbling over it each time. "Let's go," she told him later that afternoon, and together they walked over to Richard Strand's house and stood waiting at the door.

"Where's my son?" Richard Strand said.

"Out for a ride."

He looked at her, his pupils cold and clear against the back of his eyes.

"Why isn't he here?"

"I don't know. Ask him."

He pulled the door open. She followed him to the kitchen, where he turned and spread his arms wide.

"What the fuck," he said.

"I know."

"He's my son."

"I know."

"What are you doing with my son? I've asked you once before, I'm asking you again. What are you doing with my son?"

"It's beyond anything, Richard."

"What are you talking about?"

"I have no control. Zero. I wish I could explain it."

Richard Strand stood in his kitchen, by his pots and pans, by the warped, blackened things that spoke of his love for his children and asked, "Do you love him?"

"Do I love him?"

"Do you love my son?"

Anna looked away.

"I can't be without him," she said. "I tried. I can't."

"Will you hurt him?"

"Not if I can help it."

"He's my son."

"You keep saying that."

"Let's not forget how well I know you, Anna, let's not forget what I did for you."

Middle of winter, the ground solid ice, birds huddled in Siberian solidarity on power lines. She'd woken up with Eva somehow by her side and—tongue stuck to her palate—she'd reached for a glass of water on the bedside table.

"Why are your hands shaking, Mamma?"

She'd called Richard Strand, and he'd pulled a thousand strings, called in a million favors. He'd taken in Eva and checked Anna into detox at noon the same day, ahead of a waiting list so long there were people camped out with plumbing around the damn place.

"How do you think I feel?" Richard Strand said. "Go ahead. Ask yourself the question."

Anna shook her head. "I'm not drinking," she said.

"You were drinking at the *mojito* party. You were drinking at the Croquet Party."

"Not like that."

"Every time I turned around you had a glass of wine in your hand."

She stood up. "Wine is not the problem here, Richard. I'm sorry to inform you, but wine is not the problem. You're the problem."

Richard Strand slammed his hand down on the kitchen counter. "I'm the problem? My son is at the mercy of a notoriously volatile serial alcoholic and I'm the problem?"

Anna felt herself split down the middle: she lost vision, she lost touch, she came undone along some jagged line from her breastbone to her gut. She shot forward like a snake.

"What have you done for your son? What the fuck have you, as a father, done for your son?"

Richard Strand's mouth fell open. He stood like Lot's wife just out of Sodom, salt right down to the bone.

"Everything I could, I did for my son."

"Everything you could? Does that include the chick who stole his savings from under his bed? Does it include the cunt that gave him a blow job when he was twelve?"

Richard Strand grew totally still. "You're out of control," he said.

"I'm out of control? Fuck you, Richard Strand. You've done *nothing* for your son. He's a mess, a beautiful mess, but he's a mess, so don't start telling *me*."

We have children. We have children, and they're nothing we're prepared for. They come to us from the softest corners of the universe, from the breath, from the hands of God, and we raise them any which way we can. They sit in grocery store carts, eyes big as leaves, skin clear as water, prey to the great offense, the unending sin—trampled underfoot, slighted, ignored, forgotten, sometimes, only sometimes, taken with extreme precaution down the silver throat of the world in winter, the wide barge of life in summer, by men who have become men, and women who have learned to calculate the weight of a single instant before it all goes dark. We have children, and we don't know how.

Chapter Nine

At the airport in Phoenix, Eva stood out against a curtain of drab humanity like the noon sun, light streaming out of her like something by El Greco.

"Oh my love," Anna said, burying her face in her daughter's hair, leading her by the hand down a million escalators out into the wide world, where they both stood blinded by the day, Eva up to her mother's shoulder already.

"Look," she shouted, standing on the tips of her toes, describing a wildly uneven line with her hand to Anna's domed forehead. "I'm as tall as you!"

They stopped at a gas station, got gas, a bag of chips, and together they set out across the desert with music on the stereo. It wasn't until past the Apache park, where the earth met the sky among the most improbable lines, that Anna turned and said, "Eva, there is something I need to tell you."

"Mom."

"What?"

"There is something I need to tell *you*."

Anna turned. "What?"

"Look at the road."

"I'm looking at the fucking road."

Eva's little body grew stiff.

"I'm sorry," Anna said softly. "Please say what you were going to tell me."

Eva had her face turned to the window, her small hands tucked between her small knees.

"Please, darling."

Her little girl turned, ice in her blue eyes.

"Daddy says you cheated on him, too."

Anna nearly slammed on the brakes, but the highway ran like a hard, fast river behind them and there was no time for anything.

"That was before you were born," she said.

Eva said nothing.

"That was before you were born, it was at the beginning. I didn't trust your father, I didn't trust him as far as I could throw him. Once I got pregnant with you, everything changed. We were a family, a unit, and I would have never cheated on him then."

Eva shrugged, her body turned to the window, her scapula pushing up hard up against her skin—an angel's wing cut off.

"Daddy says it doesn't matter. He says you cheated on him and he didn't leave you."

Anna slammed her hand against the wheel. "Son of a bitch!

Well, you go ahead and believe what you want. I know what happened. I don't need to explain it to *you*."

"Yes you do!" Eva shot back without a moment's hesitation. "You do need to explain it to me! I'm your *child!*"

"That means nothing," Anna said. "That means absolutely nothing."

The road lay like a ribbon of fire in front of them, one more blazing thing to look at and feel and get past, on the way home. Esperanza was right, this was Indian country, there was no relief from it. Just the flat exactitude of so much rock against so much sky, the purely passive life of minerals stacked in meaningless odds against the pull of gravity, the passage of time.

Mother and daughter drove across the state border in silence. They drove past rotting trailers barely anchored on the rocky land, past rusting carcasses of cars and trucks. When they pulled up against Anna's uneven fence, not a word had been exchanged. Anna put the car into neutral.

"Eva, there is something I need to tell you."

Eva yanked her backpack from her feet onto her knees. "What?" she said.

"There's someone staying with us for a while."

"Who?"

"The son of a friend."

"What friend?"

Anna took a deep breath. "Richard Strand."

Eva's head turned with a jerk. "The boy from the party?"

"He's got no place to go. He had a terrible falling out with his father and he has no place to go."

It took a fraction of time so small for Eva to process the information and come up with the *only* relevant question that, sitting there, her mouth slightly open, Anna could not help a stab of pride.

"Where's he sleeping?"

"On the couch."

"How much longer?"

"Couple days."

"Two," said Eva, raising two stiff fingers. "Two days."

Esperanza had the table set, a bowl of Cheetos glowing orange in the middle. Eva flew into her arms and the two stood as one, Esperanza's nose buried in Eva's hair, for a long time.

"Mijita," Esperanza said with a voice nobody recognized, not even her. Anna looked around her and saw no trace of the boy's belongings. Clearly Esperanza had been busy.

"Where is he?" Anna mouthed. Esperanza gave a savage shrug and looked away. Sighing, Anna brought Eva's small suitcase to her room and sat on the bed.

She had inhabited such vast spaces for so long. She had slipped through the cracks of things infinitesimally scaled—minnow-like, minuscule, resistant to rest, to repetition, always out for the next best thing. Not even Eva's father, with his polar pull, had her truly tethered. But after Eva's birth, after the big move, not a second, not a moment had been free. Before or after drop-off, before or after pickup, in the brief parentheses of time between the two, it was Eva. Mornings, afternoons, evenings had turned into lists of met or unmet needs. The lunch box Anna delivered on time, the birthday party she lit up with a piñata, the distance she covered, the gift she picked, the pancakes whose obscure chemistry she oftentimes deciphered, the single item, plucked out of the heart of some dusty store and handed over with the tenderest smile (in return for which the tenderest smile was given)—it did not matter, there was always something, and it was always Eva.

"I *need* this," Anna whispered, her head in her hands. "God, please, I need this."

At the dinner table, things loosened, slackened some. Eva stuffed Cheetos in her mouth five at a time and Esperanza laughed, spraying the immediate surroundings with Frito pie. Anna sat quietly, drinking red wine, smiling—waiting for the crash.

"Mamma."

"What?"

"You're not eating?"

"No?"

"No."

Anna smiled. "I'll eat tomorrow."

"You haven't eaten anything all day. Espi, she hasn't eaten a thing all day."

Espi's shoulders went up. "No more Cheetos," she told

Eva. "Have some Frito pie." As Eva dug a spoon into an aluminum container of wildly tinted fat, Anna heard the door slam shut and turned around. There—motorcycle jacket on, helmet hooked on elbow, eyes large and lost—was the boy.

"I didn't know we were having dinner," he said.

"Neither did I," said Anna. "Grab a chair, sit down. Eva, you remember Jack. Jack, you remember Eva."

Eva gave a sullen stare and looked away, one cheek bulging, spoon held limply in one hand. The air grew thick with things unspoken: the pinky promise, the time away from the boy's hands, the dance of summer (the breathless turning under that blind zodiac of stars), the bright, unforgiving return.

The boy pulled out a chair and said, "I would have come home sooner if I'd known we were having dinner."

Eva shot her mother a look. "Home?"

"Eee!" Esperanza said, slapping a hand down on the table. "Who's coming to Sonic?"

Eva laid her cold blue eyes on the boy. "Home?" she said.

Anna shot to her feet. "You're going to Sonic," she said.

Her little girl got up. "I'm not going anywhere."

"Fine," Anna said. "I'm going to Sonic. Catch you all later."

The night pressed in like cold fire on all sides. It hardened and tightened and got so close Anna pulled, tires burning, into the nearest bar.

"Jim Beam," she said. "Double."

An old man with a bandanna gave her a long look. "Be careful, *hija*," he said. "There are cops everywhere."

Anna looked at her drink and said nothing.

"Take the back roads," said the man with the bandanna. "Stick to them back roads, no?"

The house was dark and, for some reason, cold, as if wrapped in some bad secret, when she got back. Eva was in her room, the boy in her bed. Anna nudged him awake.

"Jesus, how much did you drink? You'll set the house on fire."

"You're sleeping on the couch," she said.

"The couch?"

"The couch."

"Why?"

"I told Eva you were sleeping on the couch."

The boy sat up in a shaft of moonlight, his dragon tensing over his skin.

"What have you told her about us? I can't find any of my shit."

"Nothing. I told her nothing."

"What do you mean, nothing?"

"Nothing."

"What does nothing mean?"

"It means nothing. How can I describe nothing to you?"

He moved and the dragon moved with him, and he was so

warm and strong, his smell so deep and familiar, that Anna couldn't help running a hand down his back.

"Describe nothing to me," the boy whispered, gathering a handful of hair, bringing her lips to his. "Do it."

He was on the couch when Eva woke up. She stood there in her pajamas staring down at him, arms crossed, the dog like a magnet at her side.

"Get up," the little girl said. In the kitchen, Esperanza and Anna exchanged a quick look.

"Get up," she said again, her voice like a razor this time. Anna ran into the living room, grabbed her daughter by the arm.

"You can't tell him to get up!" she hissed.

The little girl yanked her arm away. "Everybody's up."

"So what? Let him sleep. He's just a boy. He needs to sleep."

"I'm just a girl and I'm up."

Anna turned to Esperanza for help. Esperanza poured coffee into a cup, walked slowly over to the couch, pushed one foot against the boy's still sleeping frame and said, "Get up."

The boy sat up, eyes unfocused, hair sticking out like straw. He took the cup, looked at each of them in turn, and shook his head. "This is fucked up," he said.

Anna felt her heart turn in its cage. What if he left? Fear crawled up her spine like an insect, settling, dark and dangerous, on the back of her neck.

"I wholeheartedly agree," she said. "It's fucked up."

"Mom."

"What?"

"You have to stop swearing."

Anna turned to face her child. "I have to stop swearing? You have to stop ordering me around. You have to stop thinking you're in charge here, because, guess what? I have news for you, you're not. I pay the bills, and as long as I pay the bills, as long as I put a roof over your head and pay the bills, you do as I say. Now go get ready for school."

There was silence in the car like nothing Anna had ever listened to, silence like a scalpel bringing down flaps of flesh, laying bare the pathetic thing she truly was.

"I'm sorry," Anna said as they pulled up to the school, the dog flattened in the back like a sheet of office paper.

Eva undid her seat belt. "I'm not talking to you," she said.

"You're not talking to me?"

"No."

Anna's head began to pulse.

"Is this a joke?" she said. "After everything I have done for you? After all the sacrifices I've made for you, suddenly I have the *audacity* to tell you to stop ordering me around and you're not talking to me? I have given you everything, Eva. Everything. I have traded my own life for yours. In fact, I haven't *had* a life. You have. I haven't. And this is what I get?"

"I'm going to school, Mom."

"You're going to school."

131

Eva nodded, looking straight ahead.

"Go to school. Go. Get out."

And she did. Her little girl got out.

At the food store, Ree was checking the protein content on a box of cereal.

"Hey," she said, "this is fourteen grams. Fourteen grams is not bad. Not bad at all."

"Fourteen grams in which context?"

Ree cocked her head. "In which context? Are you okay?"

"No."

"Is it the boy?"

Anna said nothing.

"It's always the boy."

"I don't want to talk about it."

"Oh good. That makes me very happy. What do you want to talk about?"

Anna looked around. "I don't know. Congress. The Budget. The Debt."

"What debt. We got a debt?"

"We can talk about kids. How we're fucking them up."

"It's too early in the morning for that. Let's talk about injustice, let's talk about cooking. Who ever thought I would spend my adult life cooking? It was never a possibility, I was going to run the world. Cooking was, like, something my *mother* did."

"Don't cook then."

"No?"

"No."

"Let them starve?"

"Why not? I mean, what have you got to lose?"

"It's a concept, a definite concept. Melanie should go pretty quickly, she's only two."

Anna ran her hands down her face.

"I'm in a mess, Ree, a real mess. Eva's smelling blood. She thinks he's only staying a couple days and even *that* she's not putting up with."

"You told her he was only staying for a couple days?"

"I'm afraid I did."

"Well, tell her the truth. Tell her he's moved in and she has to suck it up. I'm so tired of these kids just taking over, man. I mean, what happened to us? We were the ones. We were the ones who were going to make it all fall into place and look at us, we're under the tyranny of a bunch of five-year-olds. Tell Eva she has to suck it up."

"You tell her."

"I don't know. It might sound a little strange, coming from me."

She didn't turn right to go home. She turned left and drove across town to the church of Saint Francis of Assisi. If she were to find it locked again, if the outrage were for some reason to repeat itself, she would go to the parish office and beat on the door until somebody came. She would then take the trouble to explain that a public place of worship was just that, a public place of worship, even for the likes of her, who had long stopped worshipping that particular God but needed solace—silence and solace.

The memory of a morning in church in those early days pierced her like a lance. Eva had been doodling in her notebook—encased in the autistic shell she slipped on in great haste every Sunday before church—when suddenly she'd stood up and started singing the Hallelujah. Watching her, the sting of tears in her eyes, Anna had said to herself, *If I can give her this, this sense of belonging, I will have accomplished something. She will walk into a church one day, having lost her faith, having lost her way and—without knowing how or why—find mooring in a litany of sounds. She'll find relief, she'll recover purpose, only to lose it again, but no matter, no matter.*

Luckily, the door was unlocked and Anna walked, a sudden tremor in her breath, to a spot roughly in the middle of the old adobe church and, there, sank to her knees.

Bringing both hands to her heart she said, "Please."

Things happen, things that shouldn't, things that respect no law, follow no method, assist no function, and are, in spirit and essence, nothing but madness—the cutting loose of the individual from the collective soul. On the cold floor of the church, Anna recalled her middle school teacher—hair teased, finger raised in ridiculous admonition—declaiming shrilly, *"Errare humanum est, perseverare autem diabolicum!"* To err is only human, to persevere is of the devil. Anna nod-

ded to herself, tears falling on unyielding stone, but then felt
something turn. How could she go back to that drab life, how
could she give up the thrill of the boy's hands on her naked
back, the warmth of his breath mingled with hers? And why?
Why should she? She had the right to *life,* to an identity separate from that of her child. She had a right.

At home Esperanza had the cleaning channel on and Anna
had to resist the impulse to hug her until she looked up from
the TV and said, pure metal in her voice, "The kid's gone."

For a moment Anna could not breathe. "What do you
mean, gone?"

Esperanza shrugged. "Gone. He packed a bag and left."

Anna counted to five before she said, calmly, "Did he say
where he was going?"

Esperanza didn't even bother looking up.

"No," she said. "He didn't."

Richard Strand opened the door with nothing on his face.
Nothing.

"Is he here?"

"He is."

"Can I talk to him?"

"No."

"Richard . . ."

"No."

Anna looked down at her hands. They were shaking, so she cupped her elbows and pulled them in.

"Is this your decision or is it his?"

"For the moment, mine."

"Richard . . ."

"Good-bye, Anna," and as she followed the movement of his arm in cold disbelief, the door inched shut in her face.

Chapter Ten

Low clouds moved in, and nothing was right. Even the children—golden, supple, fleet—running on winged feet toward their parents' cars seemed to Anna distinctly insect-like in their hectic sweep across the parking lot. And her little girl advancing, eyes lowered, the weight of the world chained to one foot, punitive in her progress.

Eva opened the door and settled in without a word.

"There's reason to celebrate," Anna said sharply. The little girl sat still, slack about the mouth and shoulders.

"He's gone. He's out of the house. Are you happy? Are you satisfied? Because it's all about you, right? All about *you*."

"Mom," Eva said.

"What?"

"He's Richard's son and Richard's your friend."

Anna started the car and reversed in a hard, jagged line away from the school toward a boy she did not see with a backpack, shoes, and no socks, legs like twigs. She hit the brakes with time to spare but, within seconds, there was a man with bulging eyes beating on her window with a fist.

"Are you crazy? Are you out of your mind? You could have killed him! You could have killed my son!"

Anna stepped out immediately. "I'm so sorry. I didn't see him. I'm so sorry, Tyler. Are you okay?"

"You were going a hundred fucking miles an hour, that's why you didn't see him! This is a school, there are children everywhere, you don't tear ass around the parking lot of a school!"

Anna raised both hands. "I'm so sorry," she said, and if it hadn't been for the small boy, who slipped his small hand in his father's and, looking up with large, steady eyes, said, "I'm okay, Dad. It wasn't that close," who knows what would have happened. Who knows what the combined effect of fear and rage in a father's heart might have been.

"I see you driving like that again, you can forget driving in this state until my son's in college. You got that?"

Anna nodded meekly.

"And you can forget driving with your daughter in your car, okay? I'll make sure of that. It's called child endangerment. That's what it's called. Child endangerment."

In the car, Eva would not stop crying.

"It's no big deal," said Anna, but Eva kept crying, and there was nothing in the world between school and home, only the severed sound of a sobbing child and the slow, hard beating of an adult heart and, somehow, a steady progress past the old blinking light toward the mesa and, at the point the canyon closed in around the river, the faint cries of *La Llorona*.

Anna's *latilla* fence looked puny as she parked in front of it, incapable of holding anything in or out. Eva darted out of the car and was in Esperanza's arms by the time Anna walked into the house.

"What did you do to her?"

"I did nothing to her."

"She nearly ran over Tyler! She almost killed him!"

"Let's stop talking garbage. I did no such thing."

"Yes you did! And you don't even care!"

"*Mijita*," said Esperanza, lowering her face to Eva's and pulling her closer.

It seemed to Anna, standing there, confronted with the implausibility of a united front at her expense in her own house, that every moment spent in the pursuit of Eva's happiness, every second devoted to the task had been a mistake, an error in judgment so colossal, so dire, that no compensation would ever be adequate enough, no matter the size or shape.

"I have given you everything," she said. "Everything." And she turned and headed out into the afternoon alone, shielding her eyes from the sun as she went.

There was no music in the bar, only a kind of bruised half-light in which three men sat with drinks in their dry hands.

"Jim Beam," Anna said, pulling out a stool. "Double."

Chapter Eleven

The call came at eight in the evening three days later. Esperanza was out, Eva on the couch watching TV, Anna in her study trying to pluck words out of thin air, Jim Beam like liquid amber, liquid fire, on her desk. The phone rang, and Anna peeled out of her study and into the living room and stood there staring at the sequence of digits she knew so well.

On the couch, Eva laughed her little girl's laugh and folded a long, pale leg over the other.

"Hey." The boy's voice was thick and syrupy.

"Where are you?"

"At Tito's."

Anna nodded, her mind already at work on the intricacies of crossing the entire town with cops lying spiderlike in their black cars.

"You coming?"

Anna cast a quick look at Eva. "Yes."

"I've got to be somewhere in one hour," he said.

"One hour?"

"Yeah."

"Where?"

"A party," said the boy, like it was nothing.

She ran from room to room, picking things up, dropping them, not remembering what their purpose was, the reason for their strange location, their stubborn solidity. She considered getting into the shower but there was no time. The house seemed suddenly hostile, labyrinthine. There were rooms with things that belonged to other rooms, a closet full of clothes she could not find, a pencil for the eyes she had purchased that was gone, her perfume, a brand-new bottle of Chanel No. 19, also gone, and a strange volition to the dispersion, as if the chaos had been coordinated ahead of time for the precise purpose of driving her mad and denying her even a scant ration of human happiness.

"Get in the car!" she shouted. Eva looked up with big moon-eyes.

"Why?" she asked.

"Because we're going."

"Where?"

"None of your business where. Get in the car."

"But I don't want to . . ."

Anna swept down on her little girl, her breath rank, her eyes shot through with blood.

"Get in the fucking car," she said.

*   *   *

For a while the road lay flat and exact before her, the land semi-obscured on either side under a fraying ribbon of cadmium-orange light. The air was full of what would happen next—the approaching headlights, Eva's long scream, the swerve into the sagebrush, the flip into the night. But it's always like that, there are never any signs. We look for signs, but there are never any signs.

The engine stopped. The night closed in. Nothing moved.

Chapter Twelve

She came to in a room with pale-green curtains and gray linoleum floors. Tubes—long, slender, perfectly transparent—looped out of her nose and arms. Her right eye was covered with a bandage; she would learn in time that fifty-five stitches had been applied, the tissues tightened around her eyeball, her sight saved over many hours by the work of many hands. She would learn other things in time, but for now it was just a slow coming to, a gradual surfacing, a prolonged peeling of layers until the sick realization.

She shot up in bed. "Where is my daughter?"

A nurse holding a clipboard to her chest turned, slid her reading glasses down her nose. "In the ICU," she said.

Anna held herself up—chest heaving, muscles shaking, sweat gathering under her arms—on both sides of the metal frame.

"How is she hurt?"

The nurse put the clipboard down. "Mrs. A.," she said, "your daughter is in a coma."

Anna pulled the tubes out of her nose. She unpeeled the tape holding the needles in her arms, freeing herself as the nurse began to scream. She had her feet on the floor already, she had her eye on the door already, she was holding the nurse back as far as she could hold her when the surface of the world slipped out from under her—and everything went dark.

Hours went past before the next surfacing, the next unpeeling of layers. She was tied to the metal frame of the bed this time, bound at the wrists and ankles, unable to move an inch.

"My daughter," she said through lips cracked and swollen. A doctor approached and stood peering down at her as she tensed against her bindings, struggling to keep the white figure in focus.

"You have sustained severe injuries. You have a fractured clavicle, four broken ribs, a punctured liver, a ruptured spleen, severe concussion, and you nearly lost one eye. You cannot move."

Anna's uncovered eye was dark and wide, fixed on the back of things already done.

"My daughter. I want to see my daughter."

"Your daughter is in the Intensive Care Unit. I cannot take you down there."

A tear as thick as blood slid down Anna's cheek. How was

the doctor to be persuaded, what argument could she use to soften his resistance?

"These beds," she said. "These bed have wheels, I know they have wheels. I beg you, take me to see my daughter."

"It's out of the question."

Anna tried to reach out with one hand but couldn't.

"Do you have children?" she asked.

The doctor paused. "I do."

"Imagine that was your child. Imagine that was your little girl."

The doctor straightened, shook his head with terrible slowness.

"I would not have been driving. You had a blood alcohol content of 2.0 when they brought you in, more than twice the limit."

Some things come with a margin, you can adjust to them, move around a little, negotiate the angle of compression, some kind of correspondence. Others don't. They flatten the space between molecules and fill you with nothing.

"How deep is the coma?"

"Deep," the doctor said with a voice drained of all emotion, but then something in Anna's face must have pierced him because he added, more gently, "On a scale from fifteen to three, three being the worst, she's around an eight or a ten. She's being subjected to constant stimuli. It's all we can do."

"What are the chances she'll recover?"

"We have no way of knowing. She might regain consciousness, or she might remain in a vegetative state. We can't predict any of it. As soon as you're in any shape to move, we'll bring you down there so you can talk to her. It's very important that she hears your voice. In fact, it's crucial."

"Does she have any other injuries?"

"No, no other injuries."

Anna closed her eyes.

That night, in her dream, they were down by the river gorging themselves on sunlight, so the surfacing from sleep was as if from a fresh amputation—the lopping off of both legs at the thigh, the cut past bone, the laceration through ducts and bloodways—the pain too great to bear.

"I don't want to live," she said. "If my daughter dies, I don't want to live."

Empty words to an empty room. Time passed through a sieve of silence, faint shapes moved in and out, shadows came and went. Then Ree was there with her wide eyes, Mia with green tea. They sat on the side of the bed, holding Anna's thinning hands, watching her slow tears.

"I need a lawyer," Anna said, and the following day one came—large, freckled, spectacularly short of breath—and said, "As a two-time offender, not even taking your daughter into consideration, leaving her completely out of it, you're looking at a minimum of seven days of mandatory jail time."

"That's the least of my concerns," said Anna. "Do I lose custody of my daughter if she lives?"

The lawyer crossed his legs. "Depends. If a foster home is

the only alternative, chances are you won't. You'll be subject to frequent and random testing for alcohol and drugs for a period set at the discretion of the judge, but you'll probably get to keep her. If the noncustodial parent shows up—I understand he lives in England, so I don't know what the probabilities are—and he sues for custody, he'll probably win."

"Jesus," said Mia. "You're freaking her out. Can't you see you're freaking her out?"

The lawyer considered Mia from behind lenses half an inch thick.

"Frankly, I can't see a single reason why she shouldn't be freaked out."

Mia put her hands on her hips. "Her daughter is in a coma, isn't that enough? You want her to get down on her knees? You want her to tell you she knows she fucked up? Well, she *knows* she fucked up, okay, fella? She *knows*."

Anna raised a hand.

"Quiet," she said, her head falling back into the pillow. "Quiet."

In the sanitized stillness of the night, in the sterile hush that comes over hospitals after dark, there were never any nightmares, only dreams, and in those dreams there was the river rippling with its unseen catch of fish, the serrated edge between fields and pastures down by the old house where they used to live and where Eva used to run squealing from the cows. There was Eva's knees-to-chest crouch in the observation of insect life, sandals the size of dollar bills, a swing tied to the lowest branch of a willow tree. There was Eva's small hand in hers.

Early the morning of the third day, Esperanza walked in with a single rose in a small vase and Anna wept. Esperanza sat in a chair, head bent, elbows propped on knees.

"Did they let you see her?"

"I'm not family. It's like I don't exist."

Silence fell like dust over a single ray of slanting light.

"Her father keeps calling," Esperanza said. The two women stared at each other. Esperanza ran a hand down her face. "He's her father, no? He has a right to know."

"He will take her away from me, Espi. If she lives, if Eva comes out of her coma, he will take her away from me."

Esperanza's face was like a fist.

"Don't do this to me."

"He has a right. He has a right to know."

"Not now. Please, not now."

"He's her father. He has a right to know."

Anna pulled herself up.

"You're going to do that to me? You're going to let that son of a bitch take my little girl away?"

Esperanza stood, and there were things in her eyes Anna had never seen before, things from her childhood—dreams of a constantly receding figure, her mother maybe, who had died in detention when she was only eight, mouthing, "Come, you'll be late," as the girl scrambled forward in pursuit of what inevitably turned out to be a fistful of air. Memories of hands coming down on tables, extension cords coming down on innocent flesh, doors shutting her in, closing her out, and a place in her mind where none of that ever happened.

"You don't deserve her," she said. "You had her, she was yours, and you didn't deserve to be her mother."

Anna sat up and pulled the tubes out of her nose. "And you? What about you? Look at that punk you call your son. Look at him, with chains from his nose to his nipples, with an arsenal clipped to his eyebrows, with three charges for drug possession, three more for breaking and entering, and the prize for mothering goes to you? It goes to you?"

Esperanza moved closer, one fist balled by her side. "I had my son when I was eighteen. I had no money, I had nobody. I worked my ass off to put food in his mouth, day and night I worked my ass off. You were thirty-five, money coming out of your ears, the world at your feet, and look at you, look at your daughter in a coma downstairs because you needed a fuck."

The volume needed to come down, the pitch, the tone, the register—all of it needed to come down. Anna put out a hand.

"Please," she said.

Esperanza plunged her own hands into her pockets.

"Maybe you'll get her back one day."

"Please," Anna said, her mouth full of her own tears, as Esperanza pulled the door shut behind her.

Chapter Thirteen

A strange breakfast tray came in on the morning of day four. It was bigger than usual and had things on it Anna could not place—a slab of something pink, a layer of something yellow laid up against the bank of something nearly orange. Off to one side, something white and creamy lay quiet in its hole. Anna pushed the tray away and closed her eyes.

"You've got to eat."

Anna looked up. A nurse stood there staring.

"This?" Anna said. "You want me to eat this?"

"Honey, I don't care what it is, you have to eat it. My job is to make you eat today."

After the big move, when Eva was four, maybe five, and had broadened her food range, Anna would stand in the kitchen and make things like risotto. She'd make the broth from scratch, she'd fry the onions, she'd throw in the rice, mushrooms, fennel, bacon, wildly fragranced pepper, and over the course of many, many minutes, she'd turn the thickening mass lovingly upon itself until it gained the right consistency and taste. She'd sink butter and Parmesan into it, put the lid on, and wait a while before calling Eva out for dinner. She'd lower the plate triumphantly to the table, only to have Eva stare at it with deeply troubled eyes.

"I don't like it."

"You haven't tried it."

"I don't like it."

So Anna would sit down with a fork and the fixed intent of feeding her daughter the food she had just made. Tears would start to flow, rage would rise like a black tide in Anna's heart, Paco would retreat to some corner of the house, and only by some miracle would Anna be able to physically remove herself, sit on the toilet with her head burning in her hands, then come back and say, "You're going to bed without dinner." Until one day in October when the leaves were turning and the world was on fire, someone walked into her kitchen and said, "What are you doing feeding her risotto? What are you doing feeding her spinach soufflé? Feed her bread and butter. Feed her macaroni and cheese. Feed her cheese sticks. Feed her hot dogs. The day she asks for risotto, feed her risotto."

"I want to go back in time."

"What, honey?" asked the nurse.

"I want to go back in time."

*   *   *

Hospitals occupy the coldest penumbras. Beneath the punctuality of bedside checks, of pills administered in a paper cup, underneath the orderly insertion of catheters and intravenous feeds, lies a stream of unuttered cries and broken dreams: the home run no one will witness, the first ascent no one will record, the eternally postponed walk at the end of the garden, in the shade of trees.

At night, a pall descends and much of the pretense is lost. For every mended bone, there are two that will never heal, not the right way, anyway. For every remission, two quiet deaths. These are the numbers, they're low moans in the night.

Anna had been a sick child, she'd become familiar with the smell of hospitals very early on, but somehow, just before adolescence, every disposition toward illness had vanished and she'd been spared even the discomfort of a cold. Sickness had been a world inhabited by others, a region occasionally populated by friends and relatives, never by her. In the diseased silence of the hospital at night, Anna remembered the fear that had crowded her childhood, the dread of those early years, when she'd come to understand the triumph and tragedy of a body without a shell, eyes without real casing, skulls without plate.

Richard Strand came with flowers. He sat where Esperanza had.

"How's Eva?" he said.

"In a coma."

"I know. Any news?"

"No news."

"Is there anything . . . ?"

"No," she said, knowing what would come next.

"Anna . . ."

"No."

Richard Strand rose to his feet. "But it's not his fault."

"I know it's not his fault, but my daughter is lying in a coma downstairs, and that's all I have time for."

"He's going crazy, Anna. My son is going crazy."

"I don't give a fuck about your son, Richard."

Richard Strand stood at the foot of her bed, half flesh, half stone, as if held on invisible strings. Then his lips tightened, his eyes narrowed, he leaned into the metal frame of the bed and said, "Then what have you been doing with him?"

"Beats me."

Richard Strand looked around the room. He crossed and uncrossed his arms. He turned and began pacing. He came to a stop.

"I don't understand," he said. "Help me to understand here because my son is in a lot of pain and I'd like to be able to explain to him why he's not allowed in this room to do the only thing he wants to do right now, which is to see you."

Anna's right eye began to throb. She raised a hand to it.

"Do you know what a coma is?"

"Of course I know what a coma is."

"Would you agree with me that a coma is a pretty serious thing?" Richard Strand stared. "Can we come to this conclusion together? Is it something we can do?"

"Anna . . ."

"I have nothing more to add. I have put my daughter in a coma, and I have nothing more to add."

"All he wants to do is help."

"I'm sorry. There is no room for anything else."

At the door Richard Strand turned. "What about later?" he said.

"There will be no later," she said.

Chapter Fourteen

We run from memories, we run like hell.

Eva in the bath with a rubber toy, beating it hard against the water, crying. Eva undetected the day Anna walked in, covered in blood and dust. Eva with her back to the minutiae of frost one morning, a child enchanted by the soft geometries of snow, no hat, no gloves, as Anna locked the door thinking, *You'll find out the hard way*. Eva on her knees after her first bicycle fall, her face a mask of tears.

"Get back on the bike," Anna had said.

"No."

"Get back on the bike."

Eva white-knuckled in the backseat as Anna floored the gas. Eva aching for her father's voice.

"You'll be late for school."

"But it's Daddy."

"Tell him you'll be late for school."

*　　*　　*

There was no relief to be pried from the past, and soon the nightmares began. A judge sentencing her to life in prison; an endless series of doors behind which Eva could be heard but not found; an unforgiving horizon against which her little girl dissolved while trying to say something. The waking hours weren't much better, consisting, as they did, of a single prohibition.

"It's too soon for you to walk."

"Then wheel me down."

"We can't wheel you down."

"Why not?"

"We are not allowed to wheel people down."

"Then let me try to walk, please let me try to walk," and just as she was being helped to her feet the next day, just as she began to put one foot in front of another, concealing behind a fixed smile the nausea rising in her throat, the pounding in her skull, the door swung open and the lawyer walked in—slack-jowled, entirely out of breath.

"She needs to sit down," he told the nurse.

Gripping the metal frame of her bed—her right eye pulsating madly, every inch of skin soaked with sweat—Anna lowered herself onto the bed and watched as the lawyer extended a piece of paper. "I'm sorry to be the bearer of bad news," he said, "but a temporary restraining order has been issued against you. It was filed by her father in district court. It was an ex parte decision, meaning, it was granted in your absence. You may not see your daughter until we go in front of the judge sometime next week."

Esperanza had betrayed her. She had betrayed her.

"On what grounds?" Anna asked, her voice a whisper.

"That you'll attempt to flee the country with your daughter before a custody suit gets under way. Apparently you're in possession of your daughter's passports. I understand she's got two."

Anna looked down at her hands. There were bones there she'd never seen before, hard things coming up at hard angles in a fast-forming topography of pain.

"Flee the country? My daughter is in a coma."

The lawyer's eyes softened. "I wouldn't take it too seriously. A temporary restraining order is a piece of cake to get in this state. All you have to do is ask for one. But at the next hearing he'll have to show cause, and that won't be nearly as easy."

He'll have to show cause.

How many times had Anna foreseen this exact sequence of events and gone over the complexities of smuggling Eva out of the country the minute she woke up? She had gone back and forth on the destination, then somehow settled on a Greek island. She would open a bed and breakfast and learn to make *tsatsiki*. Eva would leap into the high blue of the Ionian sea in summer and curl up against her in the glow of a fire in winter as, below them, rows of cypresses, rough mosaics of olive groves, pines, and firs, surrendered moaning to the violence of the wind. There would be no cars, no treacherous expanses of tarmac. Her child would grow up innocent, clothed in brine and honey, sea foam in her eyes. Letters would come by ferry with the new and the full moon.

No one would know.

"It should be pretty smooth sailing," the lawyer was saying. "I mean, Jesus, your daughter is in a coma and you can't even stand up . . ."

Oh but I will. I will stand up. And if she wakes, I will take her with me.

". . . We'll just need to turn in her passports, that's all."

Anna felt a sudden chill, a cold compression of chemicals stripping her down to the primal impulses of fight or flight.

"Her passports? I'm not turning in her passports."

The lawyer brought his client's face slowly into focus. "You're not turning in her passports? Is that what you said?"

"It's exactly what I said."

"You don't have a choice."

"I do. I do have a choice. My daughter is in a coma and I am physically incapable of engineering an escape. Surely you can find a way of proving that. Surely there's plenty of medical evidence in support of that."

The lawyer's eyes grew still. "Wait a second. Are you planning to take her out of the country if she comes out of her coma?"

"No, of course not. It would be impossible."

"Any judge in this country can and *will* compel you to turn in her passports."

Yeah, but I'll be gone by then. Long gone.

"I understand that. It's why you're here. It's why I hired you."

The lawyer leaned forward in his chair. "Let me explain something. There are laws in this country."

Anna pressed her palm over her bandaged eye.

"Don't talk to me about the law. The law is supremely malleable, besides which this system is backlogged. It's sluggish and it's backlogged. At the next hearing, if the judge asks for her passports, you'll present a motion, and then another motion and another after that, until we go to trial."

"You can forget about lifting the restraining order then."

Anna laid both her hands on her lap. "I have no problem with that."

"You can forget seeing your daughter."

"I have no problem with that."

"Your call," the lawyer said.

As the door closed behind him, Anna returned to the realization she'd gained in a jail cell in some African country knee-deep in shit: never, *ever,* rely on the law.

"You used to run a manufacturing plant in China."

Ree looked up and nodded.

"Can you make me a map?"

"Sure. What kind of map?"

"From here to Eva's room. With all the nurse's stations and all the ways around them—nooks, alternative routes, whatever. So I can make it from here to there without being seen. She's on the second floor. Room 276."

"Anna, there's a restraining order."

"Make me a map."

"You're all fucked up. You can't even walk."

"But a good one, Ree, a really good one."

"I can make you all the maps you—"

"Make me a map."

They pored over it together in the morning, Anna insisting for the first time on a cup of coffee and no drugs. That night—pain like a bayonet in her gut, adrenaline tensing every neuron in her brain—Anna glided like a ghost past nurses and janitors, past double doors, vending machines, around corners, down two sets of elevators and a long corridor, to a door with 276 on it. She pushed it open. Someone stood up. Anna closed the door behind her.

She'd never seen a male nurse. This one was a colossus, standing nearly seven feet tall. He had almond eyes, cheekbones like razor blades, skin the color of dark chocolate.

"I'm her mother," she said. The nurse stood like a slab of granite.

"Sixty seconds," she said. "It's all I'm asking for." The nurse cast a glance at Eva, then motioned Anna forward with his chin.

She approached against the glare of far too many monitors until she saw her—skin like chalk, bruises everywhere, Death stalking every breath with feral cool.

"Talk to her."

Anna turned, her fist in her mouth.

"Talk to her."

"Eva . . ."

"Put your mouth against her ear."

Fighting a wave of nausea, Anna leaned down. "Eva, my love," but then there were far too many tears and she began to back away.

The nurse's voice cut through the night. "Talk to her."

"I can't."

"Talk to her."

Anna filled her lungs to capacity. She exhaled slowly. She brought her mouth to her daughter's ear and talked. She talked of the dog and of the things they would do together, how she would buy a new Scrabble board and a fishing rod and a picnic basket so they could do the river in style, how they would, finally this year, set up a stand outside the house and sell apples from their tree instead of having the neighbors come and take them all, and how this time—this time—they would actually make jam and sell that, too, and the proceeds would go toward a bigger operation, a more clever money-making scheme, and she was trying to think of what that might be when she felt a rough hand tighten around her arm.

"Go."

"Why?"

"We're out of time. Please." The nurse pushed her toward the door. "Run."

"I can't run."

"Run. Your legs will carry you."

She ran and her legs carried her.

*   *   *

In her dream the next day, it was morning before school. Eva was standing by the door with no lunch box and no shoes. Hair matted, skin bruised, she stood against the light, hollow with longing. Anna opened her eyes. "She's waking up," she said.

It took ten minutes for the nurse to come—a blinding infinity of time, seconds fastening with great leisure onto the back of other seconds to form minutes, minutes bleeding unthinkingly into other minutes, as the silence around her hardened into pure dissonance, pure pain.

"My daughter."

"What about your daughter?"

"She's waking up."

"Honey."

"No honey. Call downstairs and find out if she's waking up."

She was. Her little girl was waking up. The sun hung low in the sky when a doctor Anna had never seen before pulled a chair up to her bed and said, "What we got today was a single response to a stimulus. The next step is a repetitive response, the one after that, a differentiated repetitive response."

"A differentiated repetitive response?"

The doctor nodded.

"What is that?"

The doctor tapped the back of her hand with the tip of one finger. "Tap is a single response. Tap-tap is a repetitive response. Tap-tap-taaap-tap-taaap is a differentiated repetitive response."

"So you're tapping?"

"We're tapping."

"That's it? You're tapping?"

"No." The doctor smiled. "Of course not. But for now, tapping is Eva's only available response. The rest of her body is still immobilized."

Anna closed her eyes. "How long?" she asked.

The doctor scratched his head. "I don't know why," he said, "but I have a feeling it's going to be quick."

Anna watched Ree settle by the side of her bed. "You should have been a cartographer," she said.

"Should have been?" Ree said, wiping her tears with the back of one hand. "There's still time. There's still time. Then I won't have to cook. I'll make maps instead."

Anna let go of a pale smile. "I was going to take her to Greece, you know."

"You were going to take who to Greece?"

"Eva. I was going to wait until she woke up, then I was going to smuggle her out of the country and take her to an island in Greece."

"You speak Greek?"

"No."

"You get these crazy ideas."

"I know."

"The craziest shit."

"I know."

"It could be some disorder."

"It could be."

"The poor girl. Stranded on some Greek island. So what's next? A houseboat in Malaysia?"

"I'm thinking apple jam in New Mexico this fall."

Mia came around later that morning with bits of people's lives—the asking price of a property bitterly vacated by a friend, the improbable union of two people, the acquisition of chickens by someone in their yoga studio—a woman whose only prior distinction had been the purchase of a Porsche Cayenne SUV.

"All these people getting chickens," Mia said.

Anna looked away. "Eva wanted chickens," she whispered after some time. "And a garden, she wanted a garden. I said no to both." It was Mia's turn to look away.

"Come," Anna said, pushing the covers away.

Arm in arm, they went as if for a walk to the vending machines, slipped around the corner to the back elevator and down to the third floor, where they changed elevators. They walked, talking of nothing, deflecting stares with their seeming absorption, and came to a stop only once they got to Eva's room, Anna's breath coming out fast and hard by then. Mia pushed the door open. The male nurse was gone, a short white thing stood squat and glum in a pair of white clogs instead.

"Can I help you?"

Anna stepped forward. "I'm her mother."

The nurse considered her for less than a second. "Ma'am, you're not allowed in here."

"Just one minute. Let me talk to her for just one minute."

"Ma'am, there's a restraining order against you. I can have you arrested."

"Some people . . ." Mia said, shaking her head.

The nurse brought her hands to her hips. "Excuse me, ma'am?"

"Some people ought to stay home. Spare the world their presence."

"Me? Spare the world my presence? What about *her*? She nearly killed her child!"

"Go home," Mia said. "And stay home."

Anna woke up with a start in the middle of the night and didn't even bother with her slippers. The nurse's station was deserted as she ran past, somehow light on her bare feet. Someone did a double take on the second floor, not too far from Eva's room, but Anna kept going and no one called out. She closed the door behind her. The male nurse stood up.

"This one will have to be quick," he said, so Anna lowered her mouth to her daughter's ear and began to talk, with greater fluency, greater conviction this time, and a dim sense of a full emergence, a blessed surfacing. She'd learned from Mia that chickens could be purchased over the Internet and began debating the number the two of them could handle, the female to male ratio and, beyond that, the type of greens they might be able to grow. With each sentence came details of a new relationship to the Earth. The coop would have to be marked and fenced, the garden turned and watered. As she spoke, an idea began to form in her mind of all the things Eva might latch on to in the murkiness of her state and refuse to give up once fully conscious.

Of course in the end Anna would have no choice but to tolerate the chickens. Of course she'd be the one cleaning the coop and turning the hard ground behind it with a shovel, monitoring the growth of things she'd then feel compelled to eat, but what a small price to pay—what a paltry sum, what a trifle—for the reconstituted dream.

"Time's up," the nurse said.

Anna straightened. She said, "I don't know how to thank you—" but the giant had a finger to his lips, the door open already. She slipped past him on her bare feet.

Dr. Roemer was there in the morning, surveying the damage with unmoving eyes.

"I know I used the words 'fuck you up real good,' but I didn't mean it literally."

"Where did you get that mask, Doctor Roemer? It's like

you've got a mask on. It's like you put it on in the morning and take it off at night."

"I don't remember where I got it. All I remember is it wasn't cheap. How are you?"

"Fine."

"How's the kid?"

"She's in a coma."

"I mean the other one."

Anna shrugged. "I have no idea."

"He must be hurting."

Anna's hand flew to her eye.

"Call him."

"No."

"Call him. Let him go."

He came into her dreams for the first time that afternoon. He had shaved parts of his head and he had a patch over one eye. "I'm the one who nearly lost one eye," Anna told him. The boy slid the patch down his cheek. The eyeball was gone. In its place, a hole.

She couldn't remember his number, so she called Richard Strand.

"He's gone fishing in Alaska."

"Can you give me his number?"

"My son's number."

"Yes."

"You don't remember my son's number."

"No."

"But you remember mine."

She pressed the phone against her ear, unable to think of anything to say.

"Go fuck yourself, Anna. And leave my son alone."

She crossed the room and parted the curtains. The Earth was stretched out before her, bearing no greater weight at any latitude than that of a sleeping child.

Chapter Fifteen

The moment Anna laid eyes on Eva's father, she remembered they'd been cruel to each other many times before. It was only a matter of time before she came to a second understanding. They would be as cruel, as unloving, as uncaring this time around, with one big difference. They now had a child together, a child they both loved.

She was at the window when he walked in, a creature from another planet: stiff-collared, clean-shaven, not a granule of dirt under his fingernails. They looked at each other for the first time in years, Anna in her hospital wear, her throbbing eye, her aching soul, Eva's father in a suit cut on Savile Row. His shoes had a strange gleam, as if oxidized, his teeth a vague fluorescence.

"What toothpaste are you using these days? Or have you progressed to dentures already?"

"You look smashing, Anna, just smashing. I'm taking her away, you know."

"Go for it."

"If it's the last thing I do."

"Go for it. See how far you get."

Eva's father smiled the tightest smile.

"Only you," he said. "Only you could be standing barefoot in the most extraordinary piece of clothing, having just put your own daughter in a coma, and delude yourself that nothing other than ruin, perfect ruin, perfect desolation, perfect bankruptcy on all possible levels, could visit you between now and the time your daughter wakes up and refuses to have anything to do with you. Only you, Anna. I should stand and applaud."

"You're already standing, you fucking idiot. You want to sit down and try that again?"

"Always a pleasure, Anna, always an absolute delight. We'll be seeing you in front of the judge. Hopefully without a nappy on."

Late that evening the news came. The sun had been swallowed, a whole load of land bruised in the process. A white-coated trinity floated soundlessly into Anna's room—a doctor, a nurse, and an ancillary figure with no discernible title or purpose.

The doctor said, "Your daughter wants to see you. She wants to make sure you're still alive."

Anna covered her face with her hands.

"We know that there is a restraining order in place. We are here to escort you downstairs."

*   *   *

Heads kept turning, murmurs kept chasing her as Anna advanced, flanked on either side by crisp white coats. Doctors stopped and discreetly stared, nurses cupped their mouths and exchanged low whispers, orderlies wheeled things out of her way as, all around her, something seemed to build, a momentum meant to propel her forward, past whatever resistance the air might offer. They stopped just outside Eva's room. Anna's face was bone white, she had both hands clasped around the doctor's arm.

"Are you ready?" he asked. She nodded.

The door was held open for her, and she walked to the bed and looked down into the vast blue promise in her daughter's eyes. Two small arms reached up. Anna leaned in, cupping Eva's face with both hands.

"Mamma," Eva whispered fiercely, as if parting with a secret. "I dreamed we were getting chickens."

"I've always wondered," Anna whispered back, "why do you want chickens?"

"So I can chase them. They're fun to chase, Mamma. Can we get chickens?"

Chapter Sixteen

The courtroom was empty when she got there, fifteen minutes before the hearing. Anna lowered herself slowly into a seat and opened her file.

The restraining order had been lifted, both passports handed in. After three weeks of rehabilitation in the hospital, Eva had moved with her father into a house with open views on Dolores Road. A request, filed by her father, to take Eva out of the country had been unhesitatingly denied. A motion to deprive her of visitation rights in the absence of a definitive custody arrangement had also been rejected, so every other day at noon Anna had gone around, to the hospital at first, to Eva's new home later, with progress reports on the chicken coop, whose proportions might have fallen slightly short of Eva's expectations but whose twelve tenants showed clear appreciation by refusing to strike out for loftier spaces.

Today the judge—a rotund woman with three sets of spectacles, none of which she could ever find—would rule on Eva's request, submitted by Anna, to visit her mother regularly for the undeclared purpose of rousting a dozen oblivious chickens out of their tranquility.

Anna's lawyer came, hurried as usual, and sat puffing next to her.

"Slow down. You're always out of breath."

"Slow down? How am I going to slow down when I'm always in this courtroom arguing shit on your behalf?"

Anna smiled. They'd started out badly, she and the lawyer, but over time a genuine alliance had formed, largely thanks to the plaintiff's lawyer, who wore cologne and a Cartier tank watch, and drove up from Santa Fe in a Ferrari.

It had been vicious from the start. Eva's father had come prepared. Anna's journals—stark testimonials of drug addiction during her previous life on the equator, six volumes in total, all stolen from her study years before—had been submitted. A signed affidavit from a former nanny describing a predawn drive during which Anna, drunk on vodka, had fallen asleep at the wheel had also been presented. Another affidavit, this from one of Anna's "friends," detailing a pattern of physical neglect during Eva's infancy, had been produced in triplicate. Photographs of Anna visibly intoxicated, with or without Eva, had been numbered and catalogued in fastidious order, along with a black-and-white picture of a child blowing out two candles on a cake—one of them for good luck.

They smelled the plaintiff's lawyer before they saw him, but when Anna turned around to witness the grand entry, she found, to her surprise, that he wasn't alone. Eva's father was advancing next to him down the middle aisle, nodding in agreement while tightening his tie. Anna covered her eyes and sank lower in her seat despite the pain.

"What's he doing here?" whispered the lawyer.

Anna sank lower still. "He doesn't want her near the chickens."

"What chickens?"

"My chickens."

"You've got chickens?"

"Twelve. I've got twelve."

"You? Twelve chickens?"

"I know," Anna said. "I know."

When the moment came, the argument was made that unsupervised visits could result in abduction. Mexico had a notoriously porous border, and children had a way of fitting nicely in car trunks.

"Car trunks?" whispered Anna.

"Silence," said the judge. "Motion denied. The child can, and will, visit her mother in her own home. No need to rise."

He was waiting for her by the door. "I'm warning you," he said.

"Do me the fucking favor," she said.

"Anna."

She turned. He had the eyes of a drowning man, nothing she'd ever seen before. Still, her voice was like a whip.

"What?"

"Do you have any idea of what I'm going through? Do you have the slightest idea of what your gross irresponsibility has forced upon me?"

She closed the distance between them in two long strides.

"What, precisely, have I forced upon you? Taking care of a child? Taking care of *something* for the first time in your life?"

He did not pull back. He put a finger against her breastbone and said, "I took care of *you*. For seven years I took care of you, and you were worse than a child. You were crazy. Coming home drunk, disappearing for days, doing cocaine in the bathroom, destroying every single vehicle I placed in your possession. For seven years. And now I'm in your country, at the mercy of your judicial system, trying to keep a child from being hurt again. A child who keeps telling me, day after day, that she does not want to be with me. Do you have any idea of what you're putting me through? After *everything* you've put me through?"

"You gave me *nothing*. The whole time you were with me, you gave me nothing."

"I gave you everything."

"You gave me nothing. The day I got fired, where were you? The day I miscarried, where were you? The day I gave birth to your child, where the fuck were you?"

"I'll tell you where I was: away from you."

Their eyes locked. "Away from me?"

"Away from you. You destroy everything."

"I cooked for you. I kept your house in order for you. I carried your child for you. I was there when you needed me, and you never were. Never. Not once."

He ran a hand through his hair. "I bought you a horse. Every car you ever drove was mine."

"Keep your horse. Keep your cars. Leave my daughter alone."

"She's my daughter, too, Anna. And now answer me. In good conscience, answer me. How could I possibly leave her in your care?"

"Because it's what *she wants*."

"You're completely irresponsible! In fact, allow me to re-phrase that: you've set the new gold standard for parental irresponsibility west of the Mississippi."

"I'm not irresponsible!" shouted Anna. "I made a mistake! A mistake! It was a mistake!"

"Well," said Eva's father, "it's not the sort of mistake you get to make again."

It was still summer when Eva opened the gate to the chicken coop and stepped inside, but only barely. The season was los-ing its fiber, it was losing its voice. Anna and Esperanza sat on a bench built exclusively for an audience partial to the chick-ens. The two had never talked about it, never exchanged so much as a single word. Anna had come home from the hos-pital and found Esperanza asleep on the couch, the cleaning channel on.

"Eee," Espi had said. "You scared me."

Anna had stood over her, a wave of bile rising like poison in her throat but then almost instantly subsiding.

"Are you hungry?" she'd asked. Espi had shrugged. Anna had gone to the fridge and found it full of organic lettuce, full of spinach, carrots and beets, yogurt and tofu, and, upon closer inspection, three bars of dark organic chocolate.

"There's quinoa in the pantry," Espi had said. "And wild rice."

Anna had gone to the hospital a week later with the chocolate and a dozen roses.

The nurse on the second floor had shaken her head.

"Sorry, ma'am."

"How's that possible? He's tall. Giant kind of tall."

"No, ma'am."

"He's black. Tall, black, very beautiful."

"I'm sorry, ma'am."

"Could it be that he only works at night?"

"No, ma'am. We rotate."

"You rotate?"

"We sure do."

"You're telling me I'm crazy? You're telling me I imagined a guy seven feet tall?"

"No, ma'am. I'm telling you we got nobody like that working here."

Eva's coop tactics were undeniably clever. She singled out an unsuspecting denizen and followed it stealthily, looking elsewhere—as if on a different errand, perfectly unsullied by thoughts of capture. She came up to the plumed thing at an angle, then swooped down. The chicken squawked—a hideous sound, a death-cry almost—but over time, as Eva crooned and cajoled, it developed something close to acquiescence, settled into something close to comfort in her arms.

"Did you ever chase chickens when you were little?"

"All the time," Espi said.

"Why?"

"They're fun to chase, no?"

They sat in silence until Espi said, "What happens if he gets her?"

Anna pulled her elbows in. "I get her back."

"How?"

"The way mothers get their children back. They get their shit together."

"You think he'll let you?"

"He won't have a choice. He's stuck in New Mexico, and I will appeal and appeal and appeal until I get her back."

Espi took a deep drag and raised her eyes to heaven. "I fucked things up pretty good, no?"

Anna shrugged.

"But you didn't tell me he was all mean like that!"

"He's not mean, he's English. They have their hearts taken out at birth."

Espi crushed her cigarette underfoot. "Like they do in New Mexico," she said.

*   *   *

He came at five that afternoon. Eva was standing in the coop with a seemingly sedated chicken in her arms.

"Look, Daddy!" she yelled. Eva's father waved.

"Nice house. Very Zen but for the chickens," he said.

"I'd like to take her to the river."

"That's out of the question."

"Summer is almost over. I'd like one last trip with her down to the river."

"Out of the question," he said.

She asked the judge and the judge said yes, so hope sank tender roots in Anna's heart. She packed a picnic, put the dog in the back, picked up Eva, and together they drove down the canyon, into a narrowing world of blackened basalt, past walls of perfectly vertical rock, to the river, and there they sat on a boulder watching different currents shiver in the sun as Anna spread peanut butter on a slice of bread and Paco ran in and out of the water with a stick in his mouth. Then they surveyed the bank one square foot at a time, searching for minnows.

"Mamma."

"What?"

"You're moving too fast."

"What are you talking about? I'm practically standing still."

"You're scaring them away."

"Okay."

"Slow down."

"Okay."

Eventually they got hold of two, Fred and Minnie, soon rechristened Mack and Cheese. They turned stones and scraped the bottom for minuscule insects the minnows would grow fat on. They sat on the rock, the girl in her mother's lap, blinded by the river. Later they dragged the old tree trunk closer to the edge and set off, Eva in the front, Anna in the back, for the rings of Saturn, the shoulder of Orion. "'O Captain! my Captain!'" yelled Anna. "Where to?"

Eva turned, folded herself into her mother's frame. "Home with my Mamma," she said.

Anna had heard it said that live water healed memories, so when it was time to go she sank her hands wrist-deep into the river and closed her eyes. Later she would realize that the opposite was true, that memories themselves—meticulously preserved, often revisited—are the key to redemption. This one in particular would become a constant companion, a fixed star in the months that followed. Not the crash beneath an umber sky. Not the sclerotic pulse of the hospital. Not Eva's birdlike body under a white sheet. This. This light and tumult, this wild, wild hope.

Eva's father was sitting in front of the coop when they got home. He stood, both hands in his pockets.

"Eva," Anna said. "Go to your room."

"But Mamma . . ."

"Please go to your room."
They watched her disappear inside the house.
"The judge has just ruled," he said. "She's mine."
The sun sank a little lower. The earth gave up all sound.

That was how fall came that year.

Acknowledgments

My deepest thanks go to my editor, Asya Muchnick, and my agent, Elaine Markson. Thanks also to Alice Sebold, Allegra Huston, Kate Christensen, and Julian Rubinstein. Eternal gratitude to Jen Hart and Andrea Meyer at the Love Apple for employing the unemployable.

About the Author

Lara Santoro spent most of her career as a foreign news correspondent, based primarily in Rome and in Nairobi working for *Newsweek* and the *Christian Science Monitor*. She was born in Rome and currently lives in New Mexico. She is the author of one previous novel, *Mercy*.

ML   1-13